SCALE

An Ironclaw Novel

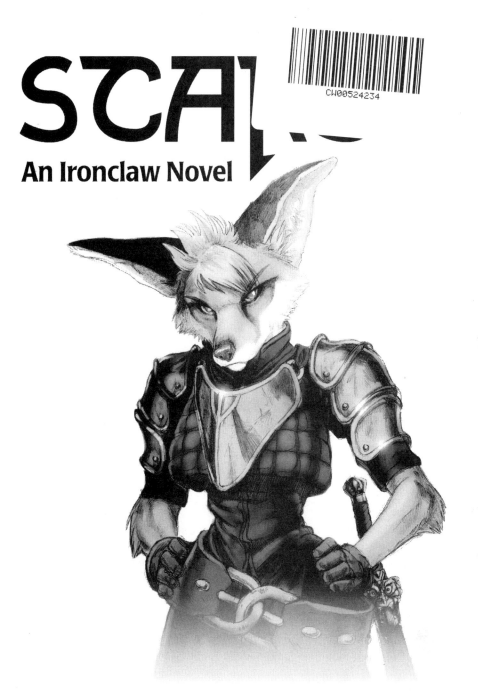

Other Products Published by Sanguine Productions Ltd.

The Ironclaw Line of Fantasy Roleplaying Games
Ironclaw
Rinaldi
Doloreaux
Phelan
Avoirdupois

The Jadeclaw Line of Fantasy Roleplaying Games
Jadeclaw

Please address questions and comments concerning this book, as well as requests for free updates on Sanguine Productions Ltd. product releases, by mail to Sanguine Productions Ltd., Rookwood Pavilion, 1-PMB-279, Cincinnati, Ohio 45208-1320, USA. You can also visit us at:

http://www.sanguineproductions.com

This is a work of fiction. All characters and events portrayed in this book are ficticous or used fictitiously.

First Edition

10 9 8 7 6 5 4 3 2 1

Sanguine Production Ltd. Publication Code SGP 9001

ISBN 0-9704583-6-3

Printed in the United States of America

To Claudia, my wife and inspiration.
You taught me to see.

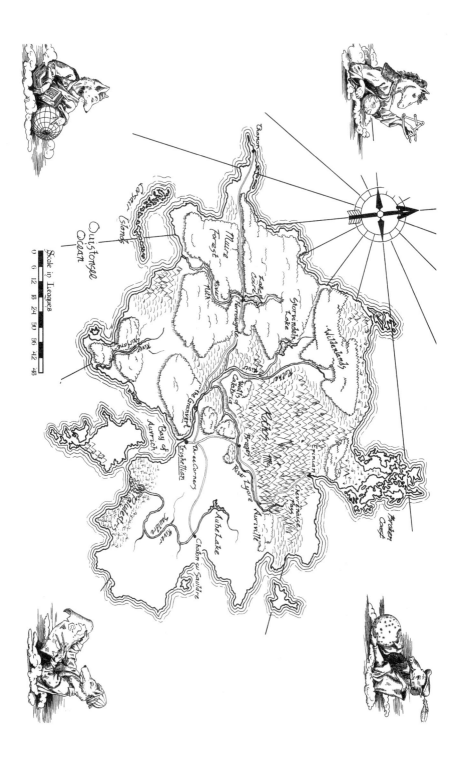

Three Spears Inn

The Aqueduct

New Town

Dock Town

Market Plaza

Cathedral de Tomoin

Old Tower

Crested Mastiff

Old Town

Shipyards

The Don's Palace

River Granvert

Bay of Auvrich

Triskellian

Chapter One

The Otter studied her eyes as if searching for a hint of her motives, her trustworthiness. She stared back, letting a small grin flicker on her lips, a faint expression of vulpine wisdom and madness coming to the fore. It unsettled those of other races, she knew; a reason the Grey Foxes of House Rinaldi held such an advantage across the bargaining table despite their relatively small stature. Being a Wizard, it was possible the Otter possessed the skill to peer into her thoughts and was attempting to do so at this very instant; she was not terribly concerned. In the event he succeeded, he would find only a firm conviction to see through her part of the bargain. Any feelings she had concerning their business were deeply buried.

"Find the Fox," he rapped out suddenly, evidently becoming impatient. No doubt to him this was a duel of wills; that was precisely why he 'lost'. "It should not be too difficult for you - people tend to stay with their own."

Not my own, she thought, studying her dusky red fur. Greys don't usually associate with the likes of me. Though all Foxes were of the same House, Reds belonged to the peasantry, not to the noble Rinaldi family. If a Grey ever bore a child with a Red, the peasant color usually dominated. It was one way the nobles managed to assure the purity of the Rinaldi line.

"My employer requires this imposter, this Pretender removed before he muddies the waters of succession," the Otter continued. "There must be no doubt, no question of his authority,if my Lord is to deal on an even footing with the Avoirdupois, the Doloreaux, or the Bisclavret."

Her smile widened fractionally. Unnerved, the Otter gave away more than when he had offered her the commission. It explained why the Wizard's charge resided in this luxurious household, no doubt owned by a friend of the Otter, rather than in his own, considerably larger domicile. He doesn't want to tip his hand, let people know he still lives. Her gaze slid down the modest hall, sweeping over tapestries depicting the ancient struggles between the Rinaldi and the Avoirdupois, the mosaic forming the scene of sainted Heloise's ascension into the Light after her final miracle, a framed Bisclavret breastplate split through the shoulder by a terrific blow. It finally settled on the perfumed fop seated with his major-domo at the marble table many paces away, framed by the end wall of the modest hall. The Grey Fox was barely recognizable at this distance. "How did he survive? Word among the masses is that Fabrizio di Rinaldi died with his father and brother." She strained her eyes, attempting to get a good look, but the heir concentrated on his conversation and ignored her and the Otter completely. With him turned half away, all she could make out was his profile.

"Incorrect." The Otter smiled, one canine winking from the corner of his mouth, the others carefully veiled. "He managed to escape the carnage, and was fortunate enough to encounter me. I was, and am more than, willing to aid him in recovering his throne and defending him against those who wish him ill. Without my Lord Fabrizio, the Rinaldi ruling family is no more, barring a dispossessed bastard or two. As a loyal subject, and one with powerful friends," this with a sweep of the arm around the hall, "it behooves me to use my influence to aid my sovereign. He has decided to take my advice and remain secluded, hidden from public knowledge until this particular situation is rectified."

Not an entirely impossible explanation, but the Otter hid something, more information, and they both knew it. She took one more, longer look at Fabrizio, then shrugged. It was not terribly important to her whether he was who the Wizard said or not, she told herself. The bounty-hunter had never taken on a job for such a sweet reward before. It was clouding her judgment, but it was also impossible to resist the allure of so much gold. "And the 'pretender'? Can you tell me any more of him?"

The Otter leaned forward in his chair, adjusting the wide-brimmed ebony hat shadowing his eyes. "Pure chance gave us a look at the man; in appearance there is a remarkable resemblance. At the time of the encounter he was with a Weasel, female, long of cloak and short of word. A Wizard, from the emanations I sensed. Oh, and accompanying them were two or three others, I cannot quite recall how many. Of the brutish sort they were; sellswords, hulking and beetle-browed no doubt. I pay little attention to such people."

She stared down at herself, slowly running her gaze over her travel-stained boots, hardened leather armor with bronze plates providing her with additional protection, heavy sword belt slung on the side of the chair. Cocking one eyebrow, she turned a long look on the wizard. Apparently the irony escaped him.

"As to where they went from that fortuitous meeting, I can only assume they yet remain in the city. Surely someone somewhere has seen something." The Otter stood, towering over her as she remained seated. "That is, after all, your job, is it not? To find those who have disappeared?" There was a challenge implicit in his words; she chose to ignore it.

"Just one more thing - why me?"

"Surely you do not think you are the only one searching for this Fox?" In a calculated move, the Mage swept both hands behind his back, pulling the heavy black cloak against his thin frame. "You are merely the first to arrive, one of many. You are well-known by the City Guard as a dependable hunter, and I heard tell you were seen in Three Corners. That is all you need to know."

Good enough. Standing as well, she reached out one gloved paw and the Otter took it carefully in the ritual clasping. Distaste momentarily colored his features; it was customary to remove one's gloves. She ignored him, accustomed as she was to such a reaction. The wizard quickly gathered up his short staff with its curious headpiece, clacking it on the tiles in such a way that the noise drew the eye. She glanced at it and away. 'Anathasian': the title gave himself, inserting it several times earlier in their conversation. The word sounded vaguely familiar, perhaps something learned in childhood. Obviously he wished her to inquire, to query him about the name or the symbol on the staff, a stylized letter A. He knew she was lettered; his request for her services had come in writing, delivered by messenger only yesterday. He was waiting for the bounty hunter to give in to her curiosity.

Danica bowed, turned, and left without a word.

*   *   *

The Don was dead.

Triskellion continued as it always had: traders moving their wares; merchants haggling in the markets, the stores, or in dark rooms and darker alleys; the occasional foreign noble seeking an advantage over another House or dueling in the shadows with the Rinaldi. New Town finely built and flourishing, bright and vital; Old Town wallowing in stagnation and decay. Life in the port city never slowed, never stopped, not even for tragedy or imminent disaster. On the surface it was business as usual, almost as though the Don and his family were still presiding over the cosmopolitan port, secure in their manor from the prying eye of the commoner. Instead, they were secure in the family mausoleum, forever unconcerned with the curiosity of the plebeians.

The Don was dead. Savagely, brutally murdered.

Danica could sense the stench of fear as she strode through the crumbling decay of Old Town. It roiled in the air, a thick miasma of unease and frustrated ignorance; the future, so calm and ordered before, had suddenly taken a swift turn into uncertainty. On the island of Calabria, four Great Houses held sway. Here in the largest city, Triskellion, the decadent Grey Foxes of Great House Rinaldi shakily held the reins of power over an ever increasingly influential and fractious Merchant's Guild. To the East the noble Avoirdupois Horse Lords controlled the plains with the might of their armies. To the West the pragmatic Wolves of the Bisclavret, youngest of the Great Houses, enriched their forested lands through innovation and youthful vitality. To the North the fierce Boars of the Doloreaux held steadfast between the other two Great Houses by sheer tenacity, as obdurate as the mountains of their home territory. All three deeply coveted the Rinaldi's wealthy lands, which included the strategically and economically vital port of Triskellion. All three knew that control over the economics of the trading city would would provide the power to catapult any House into a position of dominance over the entire island. Any of the three would have come to take it by force long ago save for one fact. Despite their decline, the Rinaldi's defenses of the city were formidable; to turn one's back on the other Houses for the length of time necessary to subdue the city would be suicide. So the Great Houses bided their time, attempting to steal through underhanded maneuvering what was impossible to wrest through force. Where a steel edge failed, a poisoned dagger might succeed. The political climate was of benefit to Danica; with stability on the island a fragile thing, there was always call for a bounty hunter somewhere. But now the situation had changed drastically.

It had been a full month since the bounty-hunter last entered the city; at the time the reigning Don of Great House Rinaldi was celebrating his second marriage, this one to a foreigner. The festivals and constant partying had grated on Danica's nerves, and she quickly left, following the trail of a wanted murderer. Danica knew

Scars   Ironclaw Fiction

nothing of the Don's new wife save that she was a Grey Fox, and thus of acceptable blood. This was probably a good thing for the Great House; inbreeding had been rife over the last few generations, with no new blood entering the Great House. Such a situation could only lead to ruin. Indeed, commoner and noble alike speculated as to whether the decline of the Rinaldi was due to their lack of numbers and their prejudice in choosing partners. The Rinaldi defended their choices by pointing out that to marry a Fox of lesser standard, one who was not Grey, would visibly taint the blood, producing red-furred offspring. So it was that recently the Don searched abroad for a suitable bride, and found her. Or perhaps not, seeing as he apparently divorced the woman before church and court not a week prior to his death.

Scuttlebutt in Three Corners, where Danica was resting when she received her 'offer', said that the new bride was something of a disgrace to the Rinaldi. People muttered about her 'bizarre foreign ways', and made veiled reference to odd customs. Some even went so far as to whisper accusations of heresy. Whatever the gossip, one thing was clear: the new wife was being linked to the death of the Rinaldi ruler. And each whispered rumor was accompanied by a worried glance and a quick flare of fear behind the eyes of the speaker.

Without the Rinaldi's hereditary rulers, the slaughtered Don Fidelio de Rinaldi and his dead family, who would deal with the Great Houses? The other, lesser Rinaldi? They were preparing themselves for a war of politics and poison over the throne, preoccupied with the desperate matter of succession. The first to claim the throne would die shortly thereafter unless he first dispatched his rivals; it was best to remove all other claimants before attempting to sit upon the precarious seat, ostensibly ruling the city and surrounding lands. The nascent Merchant Guild Council? It seemed unlikely the Lords of the Great Houses would accept them; the power of gold yet remained insufficient to grant equality between commoner and noble. And without the stamp of Rinaldi backing, without a certain amount of pride in their rulers, was it not possible that the city militia would be somewhat less devout in their duty of defense? If a man did a thing for money alone, there might be much else he could do for more of the same.... Treachery, an opening of the city gates to a rival military power was certainly not out of the question. To the average citizen of Triskellion the future must seem bleak and grim indeed.

Danica shrugged under her heavy cloak; it really was none of her business. This city had ceased to be a home for her many years before, and was now only a convenient place to make a living. She rarely stayed for more than a month at a time; her sleep suffered and waking hours were no better. Too many memories. Besides, with Fabrizio still alive the citizens would find their problem solved in time, and the city's tension would turn to celebration when he moved into the open. Oddly enough, this was quite comforting for her. After all, she considered, war would be bad for business. Items of lesser importance, such as murderers, thieves, rewards, and low justice, often paled into insignificance beside the threat of invasion, subjugation, and possible massacre. Without a stable governing body, without an acceptable ruler, it would only be a matter of time before the other Great

Houses moved, regardless of the precarious political situation among them. Better to strike first and risk failure than sit back, overcautious, and see another house reap the spoils of Triskellion and the Rinaldi lands. Danica steadfastly refused to consider there might be other reasons for her satisfaction. Best not to think overmuch about the past. The Don was dead, and it had nothing to do with her at all. Nothing.

The jagged spike of the old watchtower gave away the whereabouts of the Crested Mastiff. Shifting her route, the bounty hunter navigated through the streetwalkers on her course towards the inn, down the main street of Old Town. The aqueduct flowed steadily on her left, the splashing of men in its gurgling waters attracting her attention. Prisoners, minor criminals and debtors most likely, chained at the ankles and bearing tools and bags. Overseen by the Guard, their job was to fish the detritus and waste from the water, to keep it flowing swiftly and cleanly through the streets. Unpleasant, but preferable to the stocks or a brief stay in the filthy, disease-ridden prison. Danica looked away, unconcerned. She saw enough of such people in the course of her work; they hardly interested her now.

Striding along the cobblestones she tried to avoid staring at the massive stone keep of the Rinaldi clan, looming over the dilapidated Old Town. As usual, she failed. After several surreptitious glances she gave up entirely, turning to face the ancient monolith from an earlier, war-torn time. Her eyes flicked along the vine-covered walls, stained by weather, crumbling here and there. Now, with the choice of weapons in battle being words and treaties and the popular tactic political outmaneuvering, the slowly fading fortification offered less protection than parchment. At least you can write something on that, she mused, like a treaty. But the walls might become necessary soon, if this pretender interfered with the succession.

A small group of Old Town children sprinted by behind her, laughing and gaily singing a silly little song, cheerfully uncaring of their ragged clothing and lack of footgear. Abruptly the walls of the Keep wavered before her eyes, and the bounty hunter's memories betrayed her, as she heard the voice of another child from long ago, singing a different song. Fingertips itching, Danica rubbed gloved hands together. With an effort she regained control of herself, pushing childhood memory aside and turning her back on the fortification to regain her bearings and continue on, toward the inn. Dimly the hunter became aware her thoughts were wandering, deep exhaustion from the long journey and lack of sleep settling in. It would definitely be best to get to the Crested Mastiff. One last look she stole at the Rinadi home before turning away. It stared back, arrow slits like cat's pupils burning a hole into her back as she moved into the filthier alleys of Old Town.

Light, I hate this city.

*   *   *

The Crested Mastiff was nearly empty this time of day, with only Delaney, the Raccoon Innmaster, and Tucker, his sometime protégé and occasional irritant, seated at a table playing a quick game of Steel and Stone. Tucker stood as she entered, hip banging against the table, upsetting a game piece, black-masked eyes darting her way. On edge, Danica noted, more so than usual. Any decent burglar developed a quick eye for trouble; she supposed the tension in the city stretched his senses that much tighter. Most likely the Guard was his worry. With the death of the Don, they would be desperate and furious. A person even suspected of being a scofflaw could be in serious trouble if the Guard happened across him, becoming an outlet for their rage and fear if nothing else. Tucker had passed beyond the point of being merely a suspected thief long ago; if he was caught a severe beating would be the least of his problems.

The two made an interesting study in contrasts: Tucker, tall and rangy, full of nervous energy, with a tail that snapped like a panther's, despite its puff of fur; Delaney, massive and stout, calm and careful in posture and mien, with his own bedraggled tail half missing. It was an ugly reminder of the other scars crisscrossing his body underneath shirt and trousers. Danica had discovered them during a brawl years before in the inn, when she herself was new to Old Town and living with Delaney at the Crested Mastiff. A group of excitable young Bisclavret mercenaries took it into their heads to insult and bait several Doloreaux caravan guards when one of the Northerners stole the attentions of a pretty serving girl. Naturally the Boars failed to keep their tempers; a common problem with the Doloreaux. Young, timid, and desperate to help, Danica stepped in to smack a brandy bottle into the skull of a Wolf trying vainly to knock Delaney off his feet. Her victim took part of the Innkeeper's shirt with him as he fell, and she received one good look at the Raccoon's back before he leapt into the wild melee, tossing Wolves and Boars aside like children. It had not been a pretty sight, neither the brutal scars nor the flying bodies.

Of course, she considered, her fingers itching again, I'm one to talk. Not asking about his scars seemed politic, since he never asked about hers.

"Danica," the younger 'coon breathed. A grin widened his jaw and a sparkle lit his black-masked eyes. Sweeping into a deep bow, he skillfully parodied a noble's greeting to the ruling sovereign. Only the lack of a hat to flourish and a cloak to gather spoiled the image.

"Not now, Tucker," she muttered, frowning. Normally she put up with his youthful enthusiasm and attempts at flirtation; today the Red Fox was simply not in the mood. "I'm working."

"That's a fine hello after so long gone. I swear, none of the Foxes around here can touch you for beauty; too many of them Greys, with so little color."

Doesn't the boy ever stop? "One of these day's I'll hand you over to the Guard myself," she shot back, fondness taking the bite from her words. "But I wouldn't come all the way here from Epinian for that small a reward."

The boy relaxed slightly, leaning against the scarred wood of the long bar. A knife appeared in his hand, spinning on his palm once before dancing across the back of his fist to his other hand.

"Stop it lad! Ye may as well hang it from yer neck if ye do that." The innkeeper's accent held far more of the North than the younger man's; while they had both been born among the Bisclavret, Tucker had grown up in Triskellion. With a clack of stone on slate, Delaney shifted his Paladin, threatening Tucker's High Priest while simultaneously opening a hole in the younger man's Wall. Grunting in satisfaction, the older Raccoon heaved himself to his feet and wandered to the bar, still not having so much as glanced in her direction. "What brings ye through the door this time, Dani?"

Danica winced at the diminutive. Delaney was the only man from whom she accepted it, though Tucker often tried to use it as well. "Guess." Stepping quickly to the table, she surveyed the game while pulling off her traveling gear. It appeared as though Tucker had once again developed a complicated, cunning strategy that fell apart the moment Delaney offered him a small sacrifice. The big Innkeeper was now in the process of methodically dismantling his opponent's defenses, piece by piece. Tucker and his grand ideas; they never hold up when he puts them into practice. She dropped the heavy cloak on a chair, slipped off the sword belt with its heavy double sheaths and hung it too. Armor is too damned inconvenient, she decided, fidgeting around to find a comfortable seating. Of course, one rarely thought that way when saved from being cut open by a swift blade. While hunting for this 'pretender' Danica would probably be wearing it for quite a while. The thought depressed her.

"With the Don dead, 'tis nae a hard puzzle." The thickset 'coon plunked a bottle of brandy and a pair of cups on the gouged wood between them before settling down. He knew her tastes and shared them. Tucker flitted around the table like a bat, apparently unable to decide between sitting and chancing a quick look at her sword. Delaney made up his mind for him by dragging the burglar into a chair.

"I may need your help." The admission came with difficulty; the bounty hunter always preferred to handle things herself. But in this case, expedience was the key to gaining an enormous reward before other hunters arrived to complicate matters. "I'll throw you in for one tenth of the prize."

"Make it a quarter."

Danica fought to figure the math. Her childhood education seemed dim now, and dealing with fractions took more concentration than she had patience. Finally she simply tossed out a middle bid. "A seventh."

"What kind o'bloody share is that? A seventh?" Delaney snorted with disgust but passed her a cup, giving tacit agreement to the deal. She took it without removing her gloves. Thin stuff by the smell; not the fiery foreign drink she preferred. Free, though.

"There's a Grey Fox on the lam, and he's pretty much disappeared. Supposedly he's with a Weasel and a couple of white-shields as well. They're might be heading out of town, if they haven't already done so. I wasn't exactly given a full description of their plans." A quick sip confirmed her suspicions: definitely the cheaper local brandy. Not to complain; the price was welcome.

"A Grey? Why bother with those snobs?" sneered Tucker, flicking a finger at her rusty pelt.

"Because he's worth a very great deal of money, Tucker." And maybe quite a bit more than simple gold. It would not do, she told herself, to give away too much information. Obviously her employer wished the entire affair kept as quiet as possible, and telling anything to Tucker would be as diplomatic as screaming it from the Cathedrale de Temoin's bell tower. He lacked any sense of tact or discretion concerning other people's business.

Delaney pondered her words, rocking back and forth in his creaking chair. "All right. I'll give ye a hand on this one. Ye never can tell, I might turn summat up. After the noon rush, mind. But ye look beat, lass. Been a long trek and ye've not rested yet, I'll warrant. Why don't ye grab a room, drop your gear and take a quick nap. We'll all three get on this as soon as ye're up." Tucker nodded enthusiastic agreement.

Sighing, Danica drained the rest of her cup. Cheap though it might be, the brandy burned a path straight for her head. Delaney was right; she needed a rest. "Standard rates?"

Delaney waved his hands expansively. "If we find nothing. If we do get summat out o' this, ye'll sleep for free."

"Thanks, Delaney." Danica collected her cloak and slipped the sword belt over her shoulder. Tucker sighed with disappointment.

"Leaving so soon? I'd like to hear what you've been up to for the last month or two." His smile was wide and hopeful.

"Spare me, Tuck," she shot over her shoulder, turning away to avoid seeing his happy grin fade. "I'm out on my feet." It was very nearly true; her tread was uncomfortably heavy, and the stairs seemed nearly insurmountable. After what seemed an eternity she finally managed to reach the top, wanting to do nothing more than drop her pack and gear right there and come back for it later. Only in this neighborhood, Delaney or not, it'd be gone in a heartbeat.

The room she picked was one of the cleaner ones, without any holes in the roof; the door even shut tightly. The Crested Mastiff had not begun its existence as an inn; most buildings in Old Town ceased serving their original purpose long ago. Nobody, not Tucker, Desmond the Apothecary, nor even Delaney could agree on the earlier use of the building; opinions varied wildly. All agreed, though, that with a fair bit of work and materials it might become a decent inn. With Delaney's finances unable to support such an effort, and his will unable to bear the thought of doing the work, the result was a patch job with rooms running the gamut from decent to execrable. Not that it mattered; few travelers bothered to enter Old Town in search of a room, and the neighborhood near the old Watchtower was no place for the idle tourist. Overrun with gangs of youths and older, more vicious criminals, it was the most dangerous place in the city to be after dark. Delaney garnered the bulk of his profits from the sale of wine, ale, and cheap liquor, mostly to the honest or partly honest Old Towners, but sometimes to the very gangs dragging down the neighborhood. It was one of the reasons the local racketeers did not attempt to extort money from him. That, and the fact that the last one to try had been found screaming in an alley with two broken legs. No loss of money to crime coupled with cheap taxes, owing to the condition of the building and its dangerous location, certainly cut down on the older Raccoon's overhead.

Danica dropped her pack on the bed, and followed it with herself. *I should be up, hunting for information.* The long trek through the night had taken its toll, and burning muscles protested her every move. *I'll have to get more of those salves from Desmond.* The Apothecary was a master of alchemy, she was sure; his unguents certainly seemed magical. Practicing forms with the sword would help loosen her up; a pity she lacked the energy. Sleep was definitely a viable alternative, but there would be dreams, she knew. They were always there, waiting for her, in Triskellion.

Too bad the damned city brought her so much coin.

*   *   *

The tavern was no longer empty when she finally returned downstairs. The midafternoon crowd had arrived; lucky beggars vying with out of work laborers for spaces at the mismatched tables. Danica wrinkled her nose in faint annoyance; the sharp tang of cheap liquor hung heavily in the air. Barter flowed freely, from cheap foodstuffs for drinks all the way up to the occasional set of tools from a down-on-his-luck worker for a bottle of whiskey. Only rarely did a silver denar cross the palm of a serving girl, and then to pay for an entire table's forgetfulness, or to cancel a regular's tab.

Glancing around and looking for familiar faces, Danica felt her face split into a grin at the sight of a harried Squirrel slipping between the patrons, sporting a tray of cups. *I see Delaney's got a new girl; I wonder how long she'll last.* The drink-carriers usually moved on after a month or so; the Crested Mastiff attracted a certain kind of man most of the time, and though Delaney occasionally broke someone's head for trying to take liberties, there were only so many ribald comments and casual gropings any woman could stand. Danica often considered suggesting the innkeeper hire one of the unemployed stevedores to serve. It would certainly solve one problem.

The hunter wove carefully through the crowd, spotting the two Raccoons at the bar, Tucker assisting with the pouring and taking quick gulps when Delaney's back was turned. She shook her head; close to her in years, but still a child in many ways. At no point as she slipped through the crowd did any patron test his luck as he might with the serving girl. The regulars knew Delaney would break the bones of anyone caught in the act of bothering his tray-bearers; it failed to deter them. But the same regulars knew Danica would most likely put steel into an offending man; it had happened before. Anyone here with a friend was informed; anyone without was watched carefully on the off chance they would bring some amusement to the sour life of an Old Towner.

The bounty - hunter leaned against the bar between a pair of workers who probably outweighed her by two stone or more and motioned the younger Raccoon over. "I need to speak to you both," she said, rolling her eyes at the door. "As soon as possible."

"It's starting to thin out," Tucker replied, handing off another mug of thin ale. "And Armande is supposed to be in by now. He's running late."

"Armande?"

Tucker grinned. "Seanna brought him in - said he needed work. I've no clue where she found him; knowing my sister, I'd guess in the gutter somewhere, and she dragged him in out of pity. Delaney offered him the position and he jumped at it. He's a damned hard worker for the money Delaney pays. It's not like him to be late."

Danica digested this information. It probably made Seanna feel all holy or something. Where was Delaney getting the money to hire another bartender? "I'll be outside!" she shouted back over the din. Tucker nodded again before sweeping up two empty mugs and turning back to the kegs.

It's actually not all that loud in here, the bounty-hunter thought as she slipped back into the crowd and began working her way to the door. Normally it required constant yelling to carry on any conversation; now the noise was but a muted rumble. Not conducive to easy speaking, but.... She noted the fearful glances, the huddled groups, the lack of bickering. The familiar stink of alcohol was underlaid by another, subtler scent with which the Fox was intimately familiar. Fear. Nobody knows that Fabrizio is alive. Still. I can't believe they've managed to keep it under the waters until now. It will surface, sooner or later. Some guard will talk to a friend over an ale, and that will be that. The Otter's resourcefulness at keeping the secret up to this point certainly impressed her. It had to be him; the nobility had neither the wit nor the will to halt gossip among the servants. There must have been substantial rewards offered and nasty threats made to keep mouths closed this long.

Outside she checked the position of the sun. Late afternoon to be sure. There were more people on the streets...Old Towners hurrying to complete their errands before dark. Night in this section of the city could become decidedly unhealthy. I guess I'll have to chance it. It was unlikely she would find herself in danger; trouble generally picked less dangerous looking people to inflict itself upon. Still, Danica was glad she carried steel. The sword she slipped under the door to Delaney's room earlier, knowing full well it was one of two in the entire Inn with a lock. It would be best, with the constabulary in an uproar, if she presented a slightly less aggressive image. But not to protect herself, she considered, fingering the heavy blade hanging from the back of her belt, would be foolish. Lethally foolish.

When Tucker and Delaney finally rolled out the door, Tucker with a decided list to his walk, she sat on a discarded keg, staring at the Rinaldi Keep. The focus of her gaze was nearly involuntary. When her mind wandered in Triskellion, her eyes inevitably slid back to the slate - grey structure. Too many mysteries, she kept telling herself. That was the reason this time. No question.

"Well, the blasted Horse finally arrived. Ye'd think being related to a Great House so damned picky about manners and honor he might have the decency to show up on time." Delaney strode over and plunked himself down on the ground next to her, dropping into a cross legged position. "And Mirella quit on me; paid her a full denar to stay on for the rest of the day, so t'would be good if summat came of this, Dani." Tucker slipped along the wall until he entered her blind spot. It was hardly the first time for that little annoyance; he knew it bothered her, but continued to do it in order to get a rise from the bounty hunter. She resolutely ignored him this time, turning to the innkeeper.

"If we're going to get any of this reward, we need to move quickly. My employer suggested that I wasn't the only hunter sent for, only the first to get here. So we have to work fast if we're to keep the advantage." Danica paused, guiltily recalling the innkeeper's greeting. "Sorry to hear about your serving girl," she said, belatedly. Tucker's clothes rustled behind her; she tracked the sound, putting him directly at her back.

"'The first to get here'," Delaney repeated. "Did he say that?" At her nod his mask screwed up in consternation. "That seems odd, don't ye think?"

"I don't-" began Danica, but Tucker cut in excitedly.

"Don't we have plenty of bounty hunters in the city already he could be using? I mean, why wait for people to come from out of town? Why send for them at all?" Danica slowly turned the thought over in her mind as Delaney nodded approval of the younger Raccoon's quick comprehension. It was true. Blinded by the enormous reward she had missed that oddity entirely.

"There could be any number o' reasons, lad," continued Delaney. "He might want people with no ties to any in the city. He might want people who would nae be caught up with plottings in the city. He might want hunters who weren't already in any other person's purse. I could go on fer days. It's just an odd thing, is all."

Or, thought Danica, vague suspicion suddenly taking firmer root, he might want people who weren't familiar with Fabrizio de Rinaldi. She shook the thought off; it would do no good to speculate at this time. "The important thing now is to find the Fox." The two Raccoons shifted their attention to her at the reminder; at least she assumed Tucker did by the sounds. "The Weasel he's with is a woman, who apparently prefers to remain cloaked. She also might be a mage, so don't approach them until we know more. If you see them, keep your distance. Now I don't know what you two are going to do, but I'll head to the Keep to see the Magistrate. If he's in."

"They're stopping everyone from going in there, lass," commented Delaney warningly. "Ye may not find it easy to speak to someone."

"I'll find a way," Danica growled. "What do you plan?"

Delaney stroked his chin. "If they're on the run, and they have nae left town yet, they'll need to be staying somewheres. The only good places to hide are here in Old Town; it might be a good idea to check my competitors. I've to be back here after sundown, but that gives a few hours yet. Lad?"

Tucker shifted uncomfortably. "Well, I thought I might take a look around...see what I can see...."

Danica snorted. *He hasn't any idea what to do.*

"I doubt they've left town," she put in, ignoring Tucker's thankful look. The young burglar was obviously desperate, searching for something, anything he could do help. *They won't leave town at all if they plan on putting a pretender upon the Don's seat.* "So checking about might a very good idea. You might want to expand outwards into the New Town inns as well, Delaney."

The innkeeper eyed her suspiciously. "And why do I get the feeling that's more than a hunch, lass?"

Because it is, old friend. I just can't tell you that. The pretender could hardly hide out in an Old Town inn before making his play for power; if word got out somehow, he would be instantly discredited by the other nobility. No true noble would lay his head down with flea-infested peasants, even under the worst of circumstances, or so they claimed, and anyone attempting to pass himself off as a Lord would have to be more 'noble' than the blue-bloods themselves. It was much more likely that the imposter, the wizard, and the rest of their group had moved into a room in a decent inn and bribed the servants not to talk.

This, however, rarely prevented gossip.

"Well," Tucker chimed in, sounding inordinately pleased with himself, "if Delaney's going to check out the inns of New Town, I could save him some time by looking around here - the Old Town inns, and whatever else comes to mind. I can't hardly show my face in New Town these days. The Guard'd be all over me."

Turning slightly, Danica arched one eyebrow at him, flicking an ear in amusement. "One of your jobs got a little too hot, Tuck?"

"You've hit it right on the head there, beautiful."

Delaney reached past her and shook the younger Raccoon casually. The bounty hunter heard teeth rattle. "Don't be startin'. We need ye lookin' out for this little group, not mooning over Dani." Tucker jerked free with a muttered curse and turned away, ears flat with annoyance and embarrassment. Delaney frowned, opening his mouth to bellow, but Danica raised a finger. *Let him be,* she mouthed.

With narrowed eyes and folded arms the innkeeper stepped back, then shrugged. "Lad, there's a wee bit of gold at stake here, I'm thinking. Dani has nae told us how much, but from the look in her eyes it's quite a lot." The bounty hunter started. *Is it that obvious?*

"I'm not an idiot, Delaney." Tucker kept his back presented to them, refusing to be mollified.

Delaney obviously strained for an instant to avoid blurting out the obvious rebuttal, then relaxed. "I'm just askin' ye to keep things in perspective," he continued, evidently straining to keep the tone of his voice level.

"Perspective, sure, right," returned Tucker tensely. "Anyways, the day's getting a little old, don't you think? I'll be heading out." With that he strode quickly away, raising more than a few clouds of dust in his wake. Danica sighed. This sort of confrontation was a common occurrence between the two Raccoons of late.

"Why do you do that?"

Delaney let out his breath in a hiss between his teeth. "The lad's a dreamer; he spends his time in the clouds. I dinna mind it sometimes, but he's got t'learn to get back down here when there's work to be done."

"He's young," Danica shot back, vaguely annoyed that she felt a need to defend the young Burglar. "Give him some slack."

"Enough to hang himself, lass? Because it's the gallows if he makes a mistake in his line o'work. There's nae much difference between his age and yers." Delaney's face screwed up for an instant; an almost comical expression of annoyance twisted his mouth and dropped his ears, annoyance directed partly at Tucker and, no doubt, partly at himself. "And that's the problem, eh? I embarrassed him in front of ye."

"I don't see that as a problem," replied Danica.

"That's nae a surprise, lass. It's him who sees it that way."

The bounty hunter shook her head. "Delaney, I don't know what to do about Tuck." She began to pace, embarrassed in her turn at the subject. "I never asked for this sort of attention."

"Forget it fer now, Dani. He'll get over this little spat, and ye can worry about things between ye later." Delaney leaned back to stare at the sun for a moment. "And he was right about one thing - it's getting a wee bit late."

A deliberate end to the conversation, ironically mimicking Tucker's, but a good point nonetheless. Danica nodded slowly, and laid a hand on Delaney's arm. "Delaney - there's a lot of gold riding on this." He rolled his eyes in her direction, a spark of annoyance flaring. "Not like that, dammit. Tuck ran off before I could give him this speech, but you're still here. So I'm warning you to take care of your hide. That much gold means there'll be more people hired soon, and they won't be too picky about who they have to kill for it. It's a lot, but not worth you with a crossbow quarrel in your spine."

The scarred Raccoon relaxed at her words and parted his lips in a gap-toothed but still sharp grin. "They might be gettin' a wee bit of a surprise if they come after me, lass, but I'll be keeping that in mind." Good humor restored, he threw her a quick two-fingered salute and ambled off casually in the opposite direction from Tucker, moving towards New Town. Danica shook her head. Idiot men; they never show proper caution.

Still, she definitely would not want to be the man who decided to murder Delaney.

A quick glance around re-established her bearings. The Keep was her destination; she could be there in less than a quarter hour. Whether she could gain entrance, now that was a different matter. Best leave that 'till you arrive, Danica.

Briskly the hunter set off towards the Keep. This could very well be the largest reward she ever took in, so there was no sense in dawdling. 'They won't be too picky about who they have to kill for it'. Her words to Delaney just now, but Danica could not help but wonder just whom she herself might have to kill to earn the promised gold..

When you took a contract, you finished the job. No matter what.

Chapter Two

Dodging through the late afternoon crowds of Old Towners completing errands and heading home, Tucker fairly seethed with irritation and humiliation. Damn that arrogant, know-it-all, torn up bag of skunk excrement! Always sticking his greying snout in where it absolutely Should! Not! Be! His guts knotted as he recalled the other Raccoon dressing him down, in front of Danica no less. If only the earth had opened up to swallow the young thief; it would have taken the edge off the embarrassment. Better yet, if only it had swallowed Delaney....

A sweet scent caught his attention and Tucker stopped at a pastry cart, trading off a skin of the inn's ale for a sugar tart, cooked that morning. It went a long way towards improving his mood; he thanked the smiling Bear and continued on his way, munching happily. Now, there was a man who put heart and soul into his work; you could taste it in the pie. And why not? There wasn't a better place to live than here, in Triskellion, the largest and most lively city on Calabria. Baking pies for customers, giving out your work in exchange for goods and sometimes even money, watching the flow and eddies of the people around you; not such a bad life, Tucker decided while savoring the taste of the sticky treat.

His own life might be better, though, if Danica paid some attention to him. Well, not that she ignored him, exactly, but he'd prefer attention of a different sort. The young Raccoon broke off a piece of the tart and slipped it to one of the orphans darting through the legs of the crowd; the little mouse's squeak of surprise and pleasure brought a quick smile to his face. Smart, witty, razor-keen; all words he could use to describe the bounty hunter. Beautiful, too, he conceded, and that just made it even better. Tucker knew she presented the diamond-hard exterior to the world as a defense; every now and then he caught a glimpse of what lay behind it and it took his breath away. On that odd occasion when a crack appeared in her armor he sensed a bleak sadnesshidden deep within. Something terrible must have happened to her, for her to try to be as hard as she is.

One of his earlier resolutions had been to find a way to replace her melancholy with joy. Things did not proceed exactly as planned. Not entirely sure why the Red Fox decided he was not worth attention, Tucker resolved to simply keep trying until he wore her down. Romance, humor, assistance; having attempted all three the young Burglar was becoming more and more convinced it was persistence that would carry the day. That is, if she doesn't kill me first.

The sight of the Guard ahead, two of them patrolling through the crowd, was enough to bring Tucker's mind back to its task, but insufficient to dispel his good mood. Unfortunately a line of vision worked both ways; one of them raised an arm, pointing in his direction. Too full of energy to simply glide deeper into the crowd and hide in plain sight, the burglar dodged into one of the many small, dingy alleys riddling Old Town. They would look in here, of course, but he would be long gone by that point. Stuffing the pastry into a pouch, he scampered atop a small stack of crates, teetered precariously for an instant, then launched himself into the air.

Bouncing off a corner wall, Tucker pushed up and out again, catching the top of the shortest building with three of his clawed fingers. Feet scrabbled for an instant for purchase then caught, and he pulled himself up and over an instant before voices began to echo down the alley.

"...tell you I saw him!" One of the two guards, a Badger, ill tempered like many of his kind, kicked over the pile of crates. Tucker resisted the urge to snigger; apparently Guildmaster Rienhert still felt the sting of the disappearance of four packages of expensive spices. The Burglar rolled over and stuck his snout over the lip of the building, eyeing the guards. There was no particular concern about a chase. If by some stroke of ill fortune they spotted him, he could flee across the roofs in any of three directions, and the guards would never know which one.

"Look," replied his partner, a tall, slender equine, "we don't have time to be pulling in every single known thief we set eyes on. Leave it."

Tucker grinned. Well, she's reasonable; refreshing in a guard. He took a second look. And a much better looking Horse than old Armande.

"This whole 'keep it under wraps' order is making me crazy," snarled the Badger. "How long are we going to have to wait until we can tell people? My wife's been bothering me, and if she finds out I've been holding back...."

"I know, I know," his partner commiserated. "She'll have your hide." The mare suddenly gave the crates a frustrated kick of her own, staving one in with a hoof. Tucker winced. Then again.... "It won't be long now. Sooner or later we're going to have to tell someone that the boy's alive." Tucker's ears perked up.

The boy?

"We can't tell anyone until we find him, idiot!" The woman took the insult in stride; one usually had to when paired up with a Badger. Either that or spend a great deal of time in bandages. The guards slowly moved towards the mouth of the alley, and Tucker now began suppressing curses. He strained to catch the last few words as they paused at the entrance for an instant. "If Fabrizio..."

"Shut it!" snapped the Horse. She grabbed the Badger by his arm and pulled him, swearing, out into the street. Yes m'friend, I know exactly how that feels. Tucker slowly rolled over onto his back, eyes unseeing. Had he heard correctly? Fabrizio? Tucker only knew of one Fabrizio with whom the Guard might be concerned.

And Danica was looking for a Grey Fox.

He reached into his pouch and pulled out the somewhat crumbled pastry. No matter; it would taste just as sweet. From experience, Tucker knew it was not the packaging that proved the worth of valuables. A careful bite, and he chewed slowly while considering the implications of his discovery. He wondered what Danica had been told by her employer. Probably nothing - more likely she still labored under the impression her quarry was just another criminal type. Maybe, just maybe she might take a second look at someone who brought her this information. It was rather important, after all.

Abruptly Tucker sat up straight as a second course of action occurred to him. He rolled it over in his mind a few times, considering its possible benefits. Yes - he could very well do that too.

Delaney thought he acted like an incompetent child? It seemed the Burglar now had a chance to prove otherwise.

*   *   *

A thick sense of impending doom clung to Danica as she pushed her way through the people filling the streets, occasionally pushing aside people too slow or too obstinate to move from her path. It was a foul mood, spiced with frustration and vague annoyance...frustration with Tucker, and annoyance with Delaney. She stood tall, hoping to catch a glimpse of the younger Raccoon, but either he had too much of a lead, or had already turned off from the road to the Keep.

Why was the Burglar still bothering her? She had made it plain she had no romantic interest in him. Tucker was a friend, one of the few she had, and any dalliance between friends invariably complicated things, to say the least. And when it all fell apart, as it always did, there was another friend gone. And perhaps he would take more with him. Danica had too few friends as it was.

Besides, she told herself, Tucker can be such a child at times. Not the sort of man from whom you want anything other than friendship, indeed no.

Delaney, however, needed to keep his whiskers out of it. By barging in he only increased the friction between her and Tucker and hurt the boy to boot. It was uncalled for; the Burglar was no worse than usual today. Why had the other Raccoon chosen that moment to dole out some 'advice'? She ground her teeth in a brief spasm of fury. The next time he laid into Tucker like that Danica would...would...do something, she finished lamely. I'm not even sure why. I actually agree with the old man.

She paused by an aging Bear hawking sweets from his cart, her nose wrinkling at the sharp scent. Who knows what he puts in those things. The bounty hunter felt his stare on her back as she moved away. She never trusted street vendors, standing around all day, watching people walk by. Probably keeping an eye out for a likely looking person to mug. Certainly some of the vendors acted as spotters for the local gangs, identifying the vulnerable among the people and fingering them for the thugs. Damn, she hated this city. Full of filth, crime, and empty lives. My history here certainlydoesn't increase its appeal.

Danica quickened her pace, trying to put Tucker and Delaney out of her thoughts, succeeding only in replacing them with memories of her childhood life in Triskellion. Unfortunately, there was little improvement to be found there. Very few of her later, more easily recalled years of childhood were anything resembling joyful times. Most often remembered was the tearing bite ofexcruciating pain, the searing fire, and the final agony of abandonment. Such thoughts were always close to mind in this city.

The Keep loomed before her, startling Danica out of her ruminations. I guess I'm too used to this little walk. Still, it had been a long time since she stood in front of the black iron gates, sided by copses of apple trees littering the ground with spent blooms. Not surprisingly they were closed; the two guards in front were practicing their best glares to keep away the passers-by. Judging by the harried expressions appearing on their faces as she approached, Danica could see the tactic was not as effective as they hoped.

"No entry, no talking, no one available," sighed the guard on the left, a Red Fox like her. It had the rhythm of an oft-repeated phrase. Danica replied by reaching into a pouch and coming out with a trio of denarii, bouncing them in her hand suggestively. Both guards brightened, then sagged. The Fox looked at his partner, a Skunk, and sighed. "Look, it stands, okay? Nobody gets in, nobody talks, nobody's free to see you."

"I don't want to talk to 'nobody'," Danica countered easily, "I just want to talk to the magistrate. I'm hunting a criminal; surely he has time for that?"

The two Guards exchanged a confused look. The Skunk leaned forward slightly. "You aren't...here about the Rinaldi?"

"Should I be?" Danica waited, small pyramid of coins held on outstretched hand. They vanished an instant later.

"Wait here," the Fox instructed, unlocking the tiny door in the side of the gate. He slipped through, closing it behind. Danica heard the lock click. *I always wondered why that door was there; a battering ram would cave it in completely. Expedience, she supposed.* The color and the shape looked to her like a later addition, perhaps after the city grew up around the Keep and the threat of a siege became minimal. While she studied the door , the other guard eyed her carefully, rocking back and forth on his heels. The bounty hunter ignored him, moving away and running one hand over the slate grey stones of the Keep's wall, her black mood deepening. *Gates....*

"Be careful child," her Father's steward whispered, pushing her gently out of the entrance of the family estate. "The streets are no place for a young one like yourself." He looked behind, across the courtyard to see if any were watching, then turned back to her. "Find a farmer at the market, one who will take your coin and nothing more. Leave the city with him, and obtain work serving in whatever peasant hamlet he calls his own - this little bit will keep you until you are accepted." The Bloodhound held out a small purse of coin; she stared back helplessly, tears soaking into her fur. He looked at her hands, her agonized hands, and winced with sudden realization. Quickly the old man bent and tied the purse to her belt. "I am sorry little one. Truly. But we must obey the master." The door closed before her, swinging shut gently on greased hinges, without the hollow boom she expected. Somehow the silence was much worse.

"Dammit, Berd! This is what you dragged me out here for?" The angry voice cut through her reverie, and Danica shook her head, taking a moment to compose her features before turning. Another wall loomed before her: a massive, multicolored chest. Her eyes traveled up to the broad, purple-vested shoulders, touched briefly on the orange-sleeved arms, and narrowed at the sight of the white ruff circling the thick, grey-furred neck. Finally her gaze settled on the flat- faced visage of the local magistrate of the constabulary. *Umberto del Serio, as I live and breathe. The only* person in a thousand paces with worse taste in clothing than I. She glanced down at her travel-stained tunic, patched leather cloak, and scarred boots. *At least I can say I didn't pick them out in this condition.*

The Ape shifted back a step and rubbed his thick-knuckled hand over bleary eyes. "Danica. So the deluge of opportunists begins. Good trick getting me out here; well you've come for nothing. We're not..." It looked like the magistrate was about to launch into one of his famed tirades. Normally a fair man, he quickly grew short-tempered when frustrated or tired, and both states were writ clearly across his face with its heavily bagged, red-rimmed eyes. Danica hastened to cut him off before he built up enough heat to explode.

"Magistrate! I'm not here about the Rinaldi!"

That stopped him dead. "Hmmm? What's that you say?"

"I'm not here about the Rinaldi," Danica repeated slowly. As her words slowly began to penetrate his obviously exhausted brain she continued to lie through her teeth. "It's actually about a felon I think might have come to Triskellion, perhaps some time ago." *I hope.* Umberto looked much calmer, and the glaze was fading from his eyes; they were now beginning to gleam with the cleverness which had catapulted the Ape to his position. *Be careful - keep it simple.* "She's a Weasel, goes about cloaked and hooded. A mage, by repute. She might be traveling with a couple of bullyboys."

"A Weasel, hey?" Umberto stared down at her suspiciously. *There was no point in appearing innocent; bounty hunters were always hiding something, and she would be unable to pull off the act. She settled for looking cocky, something he would be expecting.* "Well, we did have a problem with a Weasel fitting that description about a month back. There was a bit of a ruckus at a Tavern near the docks, in which a sailor was nearly killed by your Wizard throwing fire. It seems she's a bit quick to get lethal when threatened. What's she done? Supposedly."

Wonderful. An Elementalist at the very least. "Yes, that sounds like her. She's burned down a business in Epinian, apparently. Have you seen her since the attack on the sailor?"

"We hadn't had a report until recently. A couple of days ago a patrol caught sight of her re-entering the city with some armed men. She's been spotted once or twice, even speaking with one of the Avoirdupois ambassadors, but only by pairs of constables. Their instructions are not to approach her unless backed up by a full squad, preferably armed with crossbows, and she vanishes before we can assemble a large enough group. I would have my people out after her in force by now, but with the current situation...." The magistrate's frustration at his inability to take the time to hunt down both a deadly criminal and one who must be the missing Rinaldi heir was evident in his body language. Normally good-natured and easygoing, he fairly vibrated with tension.

"What is going on, Umberto? I just got in this morning."

The Ape snorted, ruffling her whiskers. *Carrots and onions for lunch?* "I won't even dignify that with an answer. But I will wish you best of luck, Danica. The last thing we need around here right now is a Wizard willing to kill during a barroom brawl." Danica nodded in polite agreement, and Umberto took it as an end to their conversation. Which was absolutely fine with her. He vanished back into the darkness of the gates and the bounty hunter turned and slowly ambled away, giving the appearance of someone in deep thought. She could feel the stares of the guards on her back but ignored them.

The Avoirdupois ambassador. The Horselords could be behind this, of course. Would they be likely to attempt to supplant one ruler with a false one? Such a plot did not seem to fit with their ideas of honor, though Danica held the firm opinion that when times grew desperate enough, everyone's honor came second to survival or victory. That thought often kept her sane through some of the tougher decisions she made.

But the Weasel re-entering the city a few days ago, that was the most confusing piece of information. If she were involved in a plot to replace the actual ruler with a false one, wouldn't it make more sense for them to be in the city when the killings occurred? Another thought struck her and she paused, biting back a curse. If the false Fabrizio was not behind the killing of Don Fidelio and his son, it was a fabulous bit of timing on his part to be ready to step into the city at a moment's notice. It was possible that the death of the Don and his family preempted the imposter's plot to murder them, but that coincidence did stretch probability. No, it was far more likely the pretender was deeply involved with the deaths.

And if the false Fabrizio did have something to do with the deaths, why had they been out of town? Perhaps he had been hiding here, and only sent for the Weasel when the killings occurred. But if he was here before the killings, it would seem likely he would wish an able Wizard by his side for protection and help in concealment before the assassinations took place. Why would she have left the city? No doubt he would have ordered her to keep a lower profile - no spells cast in waterfront pubs. And finally, most damning, if Fabrizio was their target to replace, was it likely that they would finish his brother and father and fail to kill him?

There were too many contradictions here, either in the Otter's story, Umberto's, or both. Danica's head was beginning to ache. Enough! Remember the important thing! You've taken a contract, now get to it. She paused, leaning against a stone wall to clear her mind. Whether or not the Otter was telling the truth, she knew one thing: Umberto was not a liar. He also had more than enough reason, by his story, to want this Weasel caught. Therefore the Weasel most likely had been seen reentering the city and speaking to the Equine ambassador. It was a start.

As Danica stood considering her options, the street traffic swirling around her, she became aware of her shadow, and slightly larger one sliding up beside it. A hand fell on her arm and she stepped away, her cloak billowing out in a wide sweep to deflect any incoming blade, right hand sliding behind her back to grip the haft of the hidden weapon.

"Sssah, always the excited one, yes, Danica?" Amused, lilting, accented; an undertone of veiled menace rounded out the voice.

Danica's tension tightened a notch when she recognized the speaker. "Malik."

Same burnoose, same light brown, heavy robes, same scimitar with the well worn hilt hanging from his sash. The pungent odor of his appetite for spiced food mixed with a hint of the perfumes he always wore. "What brings you here?" A heavy sinking of her stomach came with the realization she already knew why the Coyote was in the city.

"Salaam, fair one. So quick you are to leap into business. Would you join me for a small drink?" Danica shook her head quickly. "Ah, well, I come in response to a letter from a possible client." A flick of the wrist produced the scrap of paper from a belt pouch. "As you do, perhaps? Triskellion," he noted, tapping a claw on one of his teeth thoughtfully, "is hardly your preferred local."

"Maybe," she replied slowly. "Let me see your letter."
"Perhaps after I see yours," he countered. "Perhaps we are not here for the same thing? I saw you speak to Magistrate Umberto of the fierce temper. For my part, I was not asked to meet with him. Have you been here long?"

There was no doubt in Danica's mind that the other bounty hunter was here on the same mission as she. The letter he held must be from the Otter, inviting him to a meeting to discuss a contract. Malik was an experienced hunter, and a very good one to boot. They had worked together in the past, when her mentor was still alive; Mo-gei, her teacher, had trusted Malik with his life; Danica never would. An unwholesome glitter suffused his eyes at times, a touch of murder dancing like a candle's flame in the darkness. A twisted spirit, Danica thought. The Fox knew Malik's tribe had driven him from his homeland, but he never spoke of his crime. It was not, to Danica's mind, a terribly difficult guess. Something to do with blood. Just as there was blood between them.

Abruptly she tired of the games, the fencing with words, the searching for a hidden opening. Better to lay her cards, truths and falsehoods, out on the table and let him take them as he would. It was more in keeping with the manner in which she normally spoke to people, and the longer she danced around, the more likely the devious Malik would catch hold of a frayed thread in her web of untruth. "Look Malik, I'm here hunting someone. I don't have a note. I went to the Magistrate to see if he could help me, but he's all caught up with this Rinaldi thing. I'm not going to tell you who, what, or why; this one is mine. So you go ahead and do whatever's written on your scrap of paper, and stay out of my way. Clear?"

Somewhere during her little speech the Coyote began laughing. "Oh, Danica, how I have missed you." In a rare display he actually doubled over in amusement, clutching his stomach. Passersby stared at them curiously: two hunters, one breathing heavily with frustration and anger, the other gasping for air. Heloise, I almost expected him to go for his blade. Well, not really; Malik was touchy about what he called honor and Danica as well, but he would be a fool to pull steel in front of the Keep during daylight. It would not, however, stop him from nursing a grudge and coming after her out on the road. Though he has plenty of reason for that without me giving him more. "Are you sure you will not break bread and share water with me? No more talk of work?" The smile was wide, brilliant, and like his laughter, totally insincere.

"Don't you have some place to be, Malik?" she inquired, staring pointedly at the slip of paper.

"For you, student of my friend, I have all the time in the world." Warm words, but Danica saw the emptiness in his eyes, the icicles in his smile. He smelled, tasted the lies. But she hoped he did not know where in her story they began.

"While you have time, friend of my mentor, regrettably I do not." She put a great deal of effort into not sounding mocking. When he nodded she hid her gratitude deep inside. He'll accept that for now. He has somewhere to be.

"Very well. I hope we will meet again; if not here, in this wonderful city -" now he was mocking her "- then perhaps on the open road."

Heloise forfend.

Danica watched his back as he turned and slipped through the crowd like a hunting Mastiff in tall grass. There one instant, then gone. Big trouble there;that last was a threat. She glanced around nervously, half expecting him to pop up again behind her.

"One day," she muttered. "I have one day on him. Better use it."

One day, Malik, came the thought again as she started back towards the inn with quick, nervous strides. This time it held a completely different meaning.

*   *   *

Delaney limped through the gates of Old Town, heading home to the Crested Mastiff after hours spent perusing inns. What he had seen depressed him. He knew his own business could be charitably termed 'lower class', but living there for so long blinded him to just how far the Crested Mastiff fell below what was acceptable to anyone above poverty level. By the Gods, some of them even had those new waterhouses people were talking about. If it were not for the fact that the Mastiff was more of a project to occupy his time, he might well have given up on it on the spot. Instead he simply concentrated on putting one foot in front of the other, ignoring the pain of aching joints with an ability born of much practice.

There was also the good news to consider...good for him, at least. The information he gained today guaranteed him his seventh if Danica managed to succeed in whatever scheme she had involved herself this time. A Rabbit working at the Traveler's Rest let slip a few interesting tidbits after the application of some silver oil to his tongue. The Weasel in question held a room at his inn. She and three others had been coming and going for two days now. Though they kept mostly to themselves, the Rabbit clearly remembered her mentioning their destination to one of the thugs she employed. With no tips for the Rabbit as yet, frustration etched her words firmly in the inn employee's mind. And then the gift, from Delaney, of what the servant should have received from the Weasel freed those remembered words. Just goes to show, when you're trying to keep a low profile, it dinna pay to be cheap about it. He considered the pun, and snorted. He'd been spending far too much time around Tucker.

That boy, now. He had no idea, none whatsoever, of what he was getting into. One would think that a criminal, raised in the largest city on Calabria, would possess a more cynical spirit. Somehow the thief avoided that, and it made his life more dangerous. His sister Seanna, ironically, was far better equipped in that department despite, or perhaps because of, her ties to the Church. And now the lad convinced himself that Danica was some kind of heroine out of a bard's tale. Not bloody likely. I love the lass dearly, but she's no saint, that's for sure. Few people were, but Delaney did not blame Danica for her somewhat flexible morals. She's never done anything truly despicable. He paused to consider that. Not to the best of his knowledge at any rate. Better not to ask. But it meant the boy was heading for a terrible shock when the truth came out, as it eventually would. The truth always did.

The older Raccoon recalled the day he had first laid eyes on Danica; a tiny girl, with good clothing quite spoiled by filth, sweat, and blood. Fallen prey to one of the many predators of Old Town, she was whimpering in an alley, a knife to her throat while the second man went through her pouch of silver. Who knew what they planned for her certainly Delaney never bothered to find out before stepping in. Anyone accosting a child gave up their rights to breathe, by his estimation. It was not until he brought her back to the inn that the Raccoon discovered the actual reason why she never ceased weeping. It was pain, not fear. For the next few days Delaney fed the young Fox while she healed, as it was impossible for her to hold a spoon. That someone would wound a child so viciously. Years later, his rage spent, only an abiding disgust for people's cruelty remained.

When the little girl-Fox healed sufficiently, he put her to work and kept her money in his locked box. Delaney never touched it; besides the fact that he had no need for it, the silver was hers. In the beginning life was difficult for the little girl - she wept nearly every night, and constantly eyed the door in fear, as if expecting someone to burst in and kidnap her. The innkeeper never got the full story of her appearance in Old Town, or anything else, for that matter, beyond her name. It was fine by him; there were plenty of secrets he held as well.

Then Mo-gei the Hunter came to the Crested Mastiff. And the little Red Fox left with him.

Scarcely a month had passed before the spare room was filled again, this time with Tucker and his sister Seanna. Almost seemed like I'd be opening an orphanage.

The next time he saw Danica, nearly a full year later, she had changed. No longer the quiet, injured waif, some of the softness was scoured away, calluses were building, and hard edges were forming. All in all, she learned to survive quite well. The innkeeper had not been sure the changes were for the better. Now, years later, he was certain they were not.

Delaney stepped to the side to allow old Salvador the sweet vendor pass; the two nodded to one another cordially as the Bear pushed his cart by. After spending so many years in this city, few were the Old Towners whom the Innkeeper did not know by name or by face. Much like the other residents, Salvador was not terribly pleased with his life in Old Town, but he was too poor to leave. So he made the best of what he could find and always kept his eye out for something better. Something neither of those youngsters seems to understand. They're young; they have the skill and the drive to do anything they choose. But they're so locked into what they've pictured the world as being, they can't see any other way. For Tucker, life was a wild adventure, for Danica, a vicious struggle. There were some days Delaney wanted to pick the two of them up and strangle them. At least Seanna's doing something decent with her life, despite all the hardships she's endured.

Depressing thoughts again. Perhaps he was growing old, and this was the onset of his dotage. Surreptitiously Delaney cast about for the old watchtower in the dimming light. There it was, dead ahead. At least his sense of direction still worked. Glancing around Raccoon noticed, with mild surprise, that the shadows had almost disappeared. Dark was nearly upon him. Few people filled the streets now, and those that did were either hastening home, ears twitching to catch the sound of following footsteps, or leaning against the walls and lurking in doorways, awaiting full darkness. The gangs would be out roaming freely soon. Delaney shrugged slightly, slipping off his cloak to make himself more easily recognized. Senile or not, he remained positive of one thing: no gang members with any sense in their heads, and few of them without, would go through the bother of troubling him.

As to that, very little did trouble the Innkeeper; even the loss of the Rinaldi royal family hardly made any impression. A lesson hard learned from a hard life...everything passed. And if it did not, you died. Thus, very little outside of his friends was worth any concern, beyond giving a little help occasionally to those who deserved it. Another fact of life neither of those little ones understands.

Turning the corner towards the Mastiff, the Innkeeper was not at all surprised to find Tucker seated on one of the empty kegs outside and Danica just settling down on the curb beside him. The young Raccoon held a decent enough poker-face, but long familiarity with the lad allowed Delaney to read him like a book; ill-concealed glee danced in those masked eyes. In contrast, Danica made no attempt to hide her expression as she looked up from her seat at the side of the cobbles. From her expression it almost appeared as though she had chewed on dandelion roots all day, a disgusted twist to her lips and dull frustration in her eyes.

Children. Shake them by the neck.

Chapter Three

The nightly rush finally came to an end in the Crested Mastiff, much later than usual. The city's tension once again forced those without work to bleed off their stress into mugs of beer and cups of cheap liquor. The haze of inebriation eased the tightness in their bodies and clouded the thoughts of disaster filling their minds. Surprisingly, given the number of people crammed into the bar and the tightly strung emotions, Delaney did not have to break up a single brawl that night. Not that there were none; two, in fact erupted in the crowded bar, both most likely over seating. The other patrons, however, lacking the appetite for once for further excitement and simply looking for a quick slice of oblivion, solidly and indiscriminately drubbed the troublemakers and ejected them from the Inn following the beating. It put Delaney in an expansive mood, despite his obviously aching joints; he served three rounds of free drinks, forfeiting much of his profit but gaining vast approval from the thoroughly soused crowd. So much so that when he announced his intention to close a trifle early, nobody complained. Which was probably his very purpose in loading them up, Danica thought wryly, helping the two Raccoons and the equine bartender clear the mugs off the tables. It was the least she could do for the Innkeeper. *In addition to the seventh I will hopefully owe him.* The older man hinted at useful information; Danica hoped it was better than the confusion and worry she had garnered during the day...

They settled down at a table together, leaving Armande to clean the mass of cups and mugs at the bar with a wet rag, and began to lay out their stories. Danica, wishing to avoid any possible complications, merely informed her friends what she had learned about the Weasel, keeping news of Malik and her musings over the Grey Fox to herself. Tucker only shrugged his shoulders, claiming his few hours searching had been an utter waste of time; despite his protestations, Danica could detect a febrile excitement in his eyes, and smell the nervousness in his every movement. Something obviously happened during his little search that fired his enthusiasm, something he was unwilling to divulge. As she had no real moral leg to stand upon with her own deceptions, she simply did her best to forget about it. Unfortunately the silent prayers she caught herself sending up, hoping the boy's secrets were unimportant, spoiled the attempt completely.

But it was Delaney's information, coming last, that opened up the story for her.

"You're absolutely sure your informant said Chalon de Saudre?" Merely a rhetorical question, but the news so baffled Danica, she asked anyway.

"Leaving tomorrow, just after dawn, for Chalon de Saudre. They want to get out with whatever rush there is, to blend in with the crowd. They'll probably move slow for a while, to keep pace with the mob, then speed up when they're out o' easy reach of Triskellion."

Danica mulled over Delaney's news. With the Weasel holed up in one of the New Town inns, it was obvious how she had kept hidden from the Guard. There were simply too many for the constabulary to check over the course of a few short days. With the Guard still confusion over the Rinaldi massacre, but by this time no longer scrutinizing every single person entering or leaving Triskellion, the morrow would be the best time since the killings for the Wizard and her group to escape the city. The how, when, and what made perfect sense. The most important...why...yet remained unanswered.

As Delaney rooted about for another bottle of watery brandy, Danica ignored Tucker's stare to consider that all-consuming question. It re-ignited the confusion Malik's appearance had chased away. If the imposter were truly here to supplant the Rinaldi family, then why leave? Fabrizio's continued existence remained hidden from public knowledge; were the Weasel and the pretender giving up before the game even started? Nothing in this whole damned situation makes any sense, she thought sourly. Delaney placed a half-full cup before her and she drained it absently, grimacing at the sour taste. And why head for Chalon de Saudre? Was it possible that the Avoirdupois stood behind the plot after all? For an instant she wondered if this particular contract was worth the effort; it seemed she was becoming swept up in something far greater than she had expected. But dragging at the back of her mind was her mentor's first and foremost instruction. Finish the job. Just get the Fox. Everything else will take care of itself. It's none of your concern. She clung to the thought like a mantra, repeating it over and over again, forcing down her reservations and the memories-inspired doubts threatening to resurface. The amount of coin Danica would garner from this particular hunt helped a great deal.

"Dani!" Her head jerked up to stare at the Innkeeper. "Are ye all right, lass? Ye look a bit wild about the eyes."

"I'm fine," she whispered, a dry throat betraying her. Another swift drink from her refilled cup and she repeated herself more clearly. "I'm fine, Delaney. What did you want again?"

"We were both wondering what our next step is, Danica." Tucker's eyes matched Delaney's...full of worry. For an instant their concern touched the hollowness in her chest. Sudden disgust filled the hunter then; next she would be whining at them to come and help her find the imposter. And that would not do at all - you had only yourself to depend upon, and when you began leaning on others, mistakes happened.

"Our next step? My next step is to go after them, tomorrow. I don't want to try to take them in the city. Too many people, too many chances for bad luck to strike." And the last thing I need is the Guard getting mixed up in this. If Fabrizio or his Otter hasn't told them yet, it isn't my place to give it all away. Letting out the secret might anger the murdered Don's son, which could substantially alter her reward. "You two will stay here; this is much more than I expected, and well worth your share." She decided not to point out Tucker's lack of useful intelligence-gathering; he had looked so hurt at her harsh words it did not feel right to heap more weight on his sagging shoulders.

"But you'll need us!" he burst out, somewhat predictably. "Three or four of them, and one a Wizard?" The thought struck Danica that perhaps she should not hold back the criticism; a little cut to Tucker's ego might prevent this sort of scene. A somewhat nasty retort leapt to mind, one she hoped would keep the young thief here and out of trouble, but Delaney spoke first and his words clamped her mouth firmly shut.

"Lad, how many times do I have to tell ye: leave it to the professionals. Ye wouldn't try to tell Desmond about his herbs and how to splint an arm, would ye? And ye wouldn't hearken to him if he started lecturing ye on picking a lock. Now don't start telling Dani how to hunt down this lot." The hefty Raccoon turned to her, eyes narrowing thoughtfully. "Ye are going to be fine, are ye not lass? Ye have a plan for them?" Tucker glared, obviously annoyed at this double standard, but Danica could hear the older Raccoon's underlying message to her, hiding behind the question. Lie. Tell him it will be fine. Keep him out of this.

"Delaney's right, Tuck. If I didn't have something set up already, I'd definitely let you know." Tucker spun around to face her, eyes as wide as the cup before her. She finished off its contents again, absently noting the heat beginning to trickle outward from her stomach. Even rotgut brandy'll do the trick sooner or later. "So don't worry. I'll be heading out later tomorrow morning. One moves faster than four on the march; I'd rather catch up to them than the other way around." The look he gave her was dubious, but the vague compliment threw him off stride. And why not? You don't pay him too many, the small voice of her conscience noted.

"In the meantime, I'm absolutely done in. So if you don't mind...?" Her hand swept out, replacing the bottle on the table with a denar. The Innkeeper grunted in surprise as she turned and headed for the stairs up to the second floor. He caught up with her as the bountyhunter reached the foot of the staircase, surprisingly quiet despite his bulk.

"Ye've never been a drinker, lass. Is summat up here I should know about? Or was yer last job a rough one?"

The Fox thought back to the cold streets of Epinian: the silent crowd, stunned by her announcement, staring at the man they thought an honest businessman. After all, had he not paid good money to take of the Chandlery, residing among them for some time now? She recalled the Lynx pleading for her to let him live his life out in peace with his new wife and business. 'Murder is murder' she returned, the words cutting as chill as the wind from the northern sea ruffling their fur. And the store bought with murder's profits. That thought had leapt to mind as well, but remained unspoken. Moral judgments were hardly important to the completion of her work. He wept, begged, and finally drew a knife, springing in a desperate bid for freedom. When it was over, the citizens of the neighborhood did not try to prevent her from removing the proof of his death, but they also refused to offer any aid. Even the Guard warned her to be out of town by nightfall.

All in all, pretty much an average job for a bounty hunter.

"No. It's not the last job." How to explain? I never expected this. Words he would not, could not understand without the reasons she was unprepared to give, reasons she had never given him. She considered his worried eyes under his greying mask. "Thanks."

As Danica walked up the stairs she wondered if her appreciation was for his help, or his concern.

*   *   *

It was impossible to determine the cause...a sound, a scent, a gut feeling. Any one of them could have triggered her increased heartbeat and quickened breathing; a fine edge of paranoia accompanied her vulpine heritage. There was only a single certainty to her state of being, given the circumstances. Awakening was unpleasant.

For one thing, her mouth felt as dry as her fur. A thick coat seemed spread over her tongue and from the rancid taste, her breath would be equally abominable. She had never, ever felt a greater need for some bread to clean out her mouth than now.

For another, the first thing Danica saw upon opening her eyes was Tucker, staring at her from beside the door. Chilly air raised her hackles and she resisted gritting her teeth.

"Enjoying the view?"

With a choked sound he turned away, stepping quickly over to the rude table on which lay her gear and an empty, sadly toppled bottle of dirt-cheap brandy. "I wasn't...I mean..." he stammered as Danica checked to make sure there was a sheet over her body. There was, and her gloves remained on her hands. The boy would live another day. She clasped the linen around herself and sat up, resolutely ignoring the incessant throbbing in her head.

"Who undressed me?"

Relief colored his answer. "Delaney."

That explained the gloves; Tucker would certainly have pulled them off. No more than that, of course. While she would never trust him with a secret or her valuables, she knew her virtue was safe with the boy. Whatever virtue remained to her that is.

Sighing, Danica forced herself out of bed and stumbled to the pitcher of water on the dresser. Two cupfuls later, and her stomach climbed into her snout. Only a desperate exertion of will was holding it from advancing further, but at least the pain behind her eyes would fade soon. She turned and found her unexpected visitor holding her sword, staring at the brass fitted sheath. "Tucker," she began warningly. He nearly dropped it trying to put it back on the table.

"I'm sorry!" His face twisted with frustration, warping the furry mask around his dark eyes. "I've never seen one like it, that's all."

"I've told you before, Tuck. There's no magic there. It's just foreign. Now head downstairs, I need to change." He brightened, but before the Raccoon opened his mouth her finger pointed at the door. The last thing she needed were his clumsy attempts at flirtation.

After the thief left Danica knelt next to her pack. A habitual search through her gear turned up nothing unusual; evidently she received no midnight visitors save Delaney. Good. I certainly wouldn't have awakened.

Unsteady feet made for an interesting trip down the stairs but by the time the bounty-hunter finished her breakfast, slapped together hastily by Delaney, her head was clear. The scarred Raccoon sat opposite her, lecturing Tucker about 'peekin' in on bloody guests'. That guilty party, not the least bit discomfited, plunked himself down in the middle seat.

"Anything new to tell?" she inquired, pushing the bowl away.

The Innkeeper grinned. "Perhaps a wee story. Did ye know that Lord Fabrizio might be alive?"

I thought he wasn't going to declare himself until the 'pretender' was found. "I've heard rumors," she countered carefully.

Delaney's pleasure dimmed somewhat, and for an instant suspicion glinted in his eyes. "That moneylender, Tamurello, he let slip he's been doing some business with the heir - it's nae common knowledge yet, though. But somehow the lad managed survive what killed the father and brother." He leaned closer. "I've also heard it was black magic, mayhap that new bride o'the Don's." Danica coughed and tapped a gloved finger impatiently on the table. The innkeeper grimaced. "Not one for tales, are ye."

"Only the ones in which I have a vested interest, Delaney." There was no need to find out who killed the Don, or how he died. It was not her job. The hunter's head throbbed, and only partly due to the drink. No need at all, she convinced herself.

Shifting back, the Raccoon settled his girth into the seat. "Verra well. In any case, a few things I've heard might be interesting. Salamin, that stripe - furred slaver bastard, has left the area again. Apparently he's a wee bit put out that a bunch of ne'er do wells stole into his camp and freed one of his slaves."

Slavers. I hate slavers. One of the few things Seanna and I agree on. More power to those who released the slave, but the sick feeling in Danica's stomach from the brandy began to grow again, for another reason. "A Grey Fox?" she guessed aloud. At Delaney's nod she bit back a curse. The sickness shifted into a horrible unsteadiness, as if the bountyhunter stood on the deck of a storm tossed ship, tumbling her fragile stomach over and over. This explained where the Weasel had been returning from, but if the imposter were part of a plot, what in the name of the Light was he doing in Salamin's slave chain? And if he were not part of a plot to replace Fabrizio, who could he be?

Who indeed?

"Anyways, these persons took the Fox to Tamurello's a few nights ago, on Mardi - apparently they tried to pass him off as the heir, despite him being a bit of a lackwit!" Delaney laughed, but Danica sensed his close scrutiny. She shrugged dismissively. A lackwit? "Tamurello did nae believe them at the time. The moneylender had out some kind o'reward; something to do with the estate, and needing a family member to collect money owed."

"Where did you get this information, Delaney?" That would be about four nights ago? Her employer, the Otter, must have seen the other Grey Fox at Tamurello's, then decided on eliminating him. Thus I received the letter two nights ago, on Jeudi. Quick work.

"Well, I know one o'Tamurello's cousins, see?" Delaney winked. "He comes in here to play the stones from time to time, and the moneylender took him to investigate the estate after the deaths of the Don and his son. Tamurello needed to see if anyone survived - after all, it's quite a bit o' money the Rinaldi owe him. Looks like our departed Duke was a trifle strapped for gold, and all of his festivities over his new marriage cost him a fair amount - coin he borrowed from the moneylender." Delaney shook his head, no doubt disgusted by the waste, at the money for both the marriage and the Don's divorce scant weeks later. "Tamurello found out that only two bodies were taken away, and he discreetly put out the reward offer to local people, ones in yer line of work, fer anyone with information concerning the Rinaldi deaths." He sat back again and took a sip from his cup. The sour odor, reminiscent of last night's binge, drifted across the table to Danica. It did nothing to improve the condition of her stomach. "The cousin heard about this Grey Fox from Tamurello." Danica nodded, fighting for control of her throat, and motioned him to continue. Tension combined with her hangover, and she was unable to bear it any longer. Don't let him see how much it's worrying you! "That's it, lass. Interesting story, don't you think?" Now the suspicion was evident in his posture; he leaned forward, waiting to hear what she would say about this revelation.

"This is all news to me," she began slowly. "My employer just asked me to find this Fox."

"I heard a couple of guards last night talking about Fabrizio," Tucker put in helpfully. Two pairs of eyes swivelled and pinned him to his seat. "What?" he yelped.

"Ye might have told us, lad!" snapped Delaney crossly.

"I didn't think it was important!" the burglar shot back, glancing around nervously. Short of him actually admitting so, it could not be more obvious the Raccoon lied. Delaney opened his mouth to roar.

"Anything else?" Danica cut into their argument, rapping her gloved knuckles on the table for emphasis. Tucker shook his head emphatically; Delaney paused, snapped his mouth closed, and shook his own head more slowly.

"I trust ye lass, but I think there's more here than we've heard. I'm hoping ye'll be giving us the full story when ye get back." The tone brooked no argument. Danica nodded slowly again, reluctant to agree but unable to do anything else; if she ever did figure out what was going on (and she had a nasty feeling her mind was unraveling the tangle, like it or not) she would certainly give him as much of the story as she dared. If not, the bountyhunter would make something up he could accept. "Fer now, if ye hope to be catching up to yer quarry, ye might want to be on the road."

Danica did curse this time, pushing herself out of the chair and reaching for her cloak. Delaney's hand shot out and snagged her wrist in an iron grip. "One more thing. Whatever yer not telling us is on yer mind here, lass, and it's on strong. Sure it is ye aren't at yer best if I can just reach out and take hold of ye." Danica stared down at his fingers chaining her arm in consternation. It was true; her reactions were usually far quicker. Between the hangover and her preoccupation with the mysteries of this job, not to mention her usual, Triskellion-inspired dreams, she certainly did not feel top shelf. "All the gold in the world'll do ye no good if ye're lying face down in a ditch with a bodkin in yer back." Tucker's lips thinned at that, and a faint look of determination crossed his face, there and gone like a shadow. "Now they don't have a big lead on ye, despite the hour. Patience is a virtue few manage to achieve. Truth knows the lad has nae figured that part out." The innkeeper released her wrist, one finger uncurling at a time. "Dinna get yerself killed."

A sick self-disgust filled her as she met his eyes; if not actively deceiving her friends, she certainly lied by omission. "I need to go. Now." Danica spun around, clutched her head with a whimper, then reeled towards the stairs and her gear. "Can you have some food packed for me when I come down?"

"'Tis already done, lass."

*   *   *

The city thrummed as Danica left, vibrating with a curious energy just below the limit of the senses and only felt at the edges of consciousness. The Don was still dead, and the situation not changed to the eye from the day before. Now there was rumor though, hope, a breeze of a story whispered from ear to ear. Perhaps the Rinaldi were not all lost. Perhaps someone would step forward to take up the reins of power, someone acceptable to commoner, soldier, guildmaster and noble alike. Perhaps the status quo could be preserved... and the city's safety as well. People hurried from door to door, backs still hunched with tension, but there was anxious life filling their movement rather than tight despair. The fear of potential doom was now tempered by the anticipation of possible miracles.

The bounty hunter left as soon as she was able, taking with her Delaney's packed foodstuffs for quick eating on the road. Likely as not there would be no stopping at inns. When in pursuit of prey, it paid to keep moving from dawn to dusk. If that meant being caught out on the road at nightfall, with no traveler's lodgings in sight, so be it. Walk through the dark, or bed down where you found yourself; those were the choices.

It was cool on the East Road today, but that was a pleasure and a gift for Danica's aching skull. Never again, she promised. Delaney was right, unlike many bounty hunters, she was hardly a heavy drinker. Even had she not witnessed first hand the price one paid, alcohol simply failed to agree with her, neither as recreation nor as an escape from her past. Now, through the nagging pain and nausea of a well-deserved hangover, the old memories still returned to haunt her.

"Enough!" her father bellowed, and she cowered back against the cold wall, trying to find some place, some way to escape his terrible anger. "Is this how you repay my generosity? My care?" He grasped his youngest son's face again, staring furiously into the savage gashes torn through fur into flesh and blood, slicing across the horrifying ruin of an eye. The boy whimpered in agony but held his tongue. That bravery warmed the girl's heart with pride for an instant, before shame brought ice to replace the heat. Shame at the sticky matting of the fur of her paw. Her brother's blood.

"You hate him! You always have, though he has given you naught but love!" Raging now, her father hoisted her into the air and slammed her slight frame into the wall. His ever-unpredictable temper erupted volcanically this time. With good reason. "How could you? How DARE you?"

"Father, no!" she gasped. I was angry. We were wrestling. Children's games, and I slipped. A thousand things and more to say, but none of them came, because they were all lies, because it was her fault and her fault alone. Her own anger, a gift from her father, brought her here. I could never hurt him; I love him!

The falsity of that too lay bleeding before her. Shame held her tongue in an iron grip.

"It was an accident," wailed her torn brother; "Dani didn't mean it...." Silent in his pain but crying out in his sister's defense. She could have wept then, with him so badly rent by her own claws and still thinking only of her. But their father ignored his words, shouting over the thin, weak voice.

"You have always had a temper, child, but this? THIS?" He tossed her small body aside, and she groveled on the ground, desperate to avoid his fury. "You sicken me!"

"Sicken me!"

Danica coughed, clearing her throat, and glanced about. The East road was by no means deserted; she had already passed a merchant train heading for Avoirdupois lands, a group of tradesmen and several farmers in carts. Alone and hunting, the Red Fox moved much more quickly than the herd, but that small dot behind her had kept a steady distance for the past quarter day after leaving the city. The black object remained just far enough away to blur details, determinedly dogging her footsteps. Stopping abruptly she turned and waited. It seemed to grow nearer for a short time, then halted as well. Following me. Well, it could be any number of people, but I'd split my guesses between two.

While still within the Rinaldi farmlands proper, with her quarry also on foot Danica felt she had gained a great deal of distance on them. The hunter was quicker when following an unsuspecting target; a single person traveled faster than a many. In groups, people moved only as quickly as the slowest member, even if they encouraged that person to speed up. A hunter, with her target before her, instinctively sped up to bring it down. These were simple facts from the teachings of Mo-gei. She considered the albino Leopard for an instant, the foreigner generally acknowledged by bounty hunters as the best they could think of without going back a few decades. Wherever you are, I hope the women are finer than the one who killed you.

She glanced to the side, over the many acres of fields from which the Rinaldi drew some of their taxes; beautiful, ordered, and requiring terribly hard work. The peasants worked day and night, enduring foul weather, fierce reptiles, and the occasional scofflaw. Hunting those same scofflaws had turned out to be a difficult method of making a living, but by the time Danica had discovered that fact, she realized she never possessed the courage or the strength to become a farmer.

Thinking about the Rinaldi and their lands drew her mind inexorably back to what Delaney mentioned about the imposter. "Lack-wit," she muttered to herself. On the one hand, it made sense. If the imposter simply stood as a front for another, or for a group of people, why put a clever person on the throne; such a man could prove to be dangerous. Far easier...and safer...to manipulate a fool.

But if one thought a bit deeper, all sorts of problems began to crawl from the woodwork. How could a fool deal with the other noble Great Houses? How could a fool act the part? And worst of all, how could a fool be convincing as Fabrizio di Rinaldi? Danica knew the Don's son was no idiot; quite the opposite, in fact. All those who knew anything about the family, be they peasants or merchants, and especially the other Great Houses, would be aware of that fact. Yet another piece of the curious puzzle Danica was beginning to sort out and put together in her head. A dim image of the truth began to take form; unfortunately with the information she held, it was unlikely the Red Fox would see the entire picture until the pretender fell into her hands and she could question him at length. That is, should she wish to make the effort.

Now the day grew dim, the light filtering through the low hanging carpet of clouds more and more feeble with each passing mile. After traveling for most of the hours of daylight, the bounty hunter had made up time on her quarry; now she needed rest. Her previous travels of two days ago and her heavy drinking the night before left her body ready to drop and her mind clouded and disjointed. It would not do to reach her goal on the morrow in a state of exhaustion. A good night's sleep was called for. But, Danica considered dryly, not before she took care of a nagging problem. Picking up weary feet, she quickened her pace. A leg in the trail a quarter mile ahead, where it passed through a large copse of poplars marking the edges of two fields, would be the perfect place to deal with her pursuer.

*   *   *

The expression on his face when she rose up from concealment behind the half-rotted hollow log was glorious to behold. Shock, consternation, embarrassment, frustration, and yes, even a little fear chased each other across his features. "Tucker," Danica growled as he backed up a pace, hands instinctively rising in a soothing gesture, "I've one question. How much a fool do you think I am?" Stepping back onto the track the Fox brushed leaves from her arm, and awaited his response. Nothing like opening a conversation with a question for which there's no right answer. A good strategy - always begin with a solid advantage.

If her other suspicion had been correct and it was Malik following her, Danica had no idea how the situation might have played out. Would she have ambushed him? Called out to him, asked to split the reward? No, definitely not that. Tried to lead him off? The only thing the Fox knew beyond a doubt was that she could ill afford him at her back and the Coyote would certainly not have missed her hiding behind the log.

Tucker's mouth widened with a roguish grin; unfortunately for him, Danica was old enough that it had little effect. Old enough in my heart, anyway. With a scuffle of feet he gained another pace between them. "That's it? No 'how was the walk, Tuck?' No 'what are you doing here, Tuck?'" the burglar asked, obviously trying to gain a bit more time while considering his options. As he glanced to his left and right the bounty hunter almost laughed; the young burglar certainly missed the city and its easy escape routes. A fish out of water, here. His eyes met Danica's and he shrugged helplessly.

Danica covered the space between them in three quickstrides. With the hangover mostly worn off she was nearly her old self, if a trifle stiff from the travel. He barely had time to flinch before she hooked his collar in her gloved hands. Bringing his snout down to hers, Danica glared into his dark eyes. No doubt under other circumstances he would be enjoying the attention. Now, however, his twitching told her Tucker might have finally realized just how annoyed she actually was. "I don't ask useless questions." Bigger, perhaps stronger, but the Raccoon was frightened, on the defensive, and Danica had plenty of experience dragging around large men. Quickly she stepped close, shoving one leg between his two, throwing him off balance completely; to an observer, it would resemble the opening move for some kind of salacious dance. From there, it was easy to manhandle him, yelping and squirming, across the road and slam his backside down on the log. The Fox chose the driest looking section, out of a faint admiration for his tenacity if nothing else. Maybe the smile works on me better than I thought. Tucker tried to stand, but an open palm against his chest dropped him back down to his seat. He chittered briefly in annoyance before settling with a persecuted expression.

"You aren't coming with me, Tucker." One look in his eyes and she knew it was hopeless, but Danica had to try. Oh Heloise, he has this one between his teeth.

"C'mon, Dani...Danica," he amended hastily at her steely glare. She let go of the hilt of her knife one finger at a time. "How do you know you won't need help? Bloody Truth, there's three of them and a Wizard. Plus the Fox, and you can bet gold against swill he'll help them if a bounty hunter turns up looking for his hide."

Maybe he will, at that. Even if her growing suspicions about the Grey Fox proved correct. "The mage will be no problem if I catch her off guard," she muttered, "and I've handled four to one odds before." Of course you have, Danica. You handled them so well the survivor left you with the dead. She managed to shake off that particular memory and continued, desperately hoping to dissuade him. "Tucker, this isn't a poem, or a song." Catching his wistful look she added: "Or a bad romance play." He deflated slightly. "This is real. And you... you've no experience at all."

"I'm rather successful at what I do, you know." He tried to sound haughty and injured, but it came out with a hint of whine. Truth be told, Tucker excelled well enough at his calling to still enjoy the freedom of walking the streets, never having been caught. Most other thieves would have been in and out of the stocks, or worse, by now. But this sort of business, the deadly type, was a different matter altogether. With no experience, many misconceptions, and a terribly wrong personality, the

Raccoon could be a dangerous liability. He's never even killed someone. Heloise
forgive me for thinking that.

"You never even saw me, and I'm not such a good hand at hiding, Tuck. You
don't have anything packed, Light's sake. Did you even think to bring food?"
Abruptly Danica snagged her backpack from behind the log and began to march
quickly down the cobbled road. After the long day the leather sack felt brutally
heavy; she needed to find a good place for rest immediately. After a moment the
bounty hunter heard Tucker scramble to his feet and scurry after her. Send him
back at knife's point and have him wander about after me in the dark, or keep him
close and easy to watch. It was an easy choice to make. Besides, the idea of pulling
steel on the burglar, even as a threat, did not sit well at all. "Come on, hurry up.
We have to find somewhere sheltered before dark so they won't be able to see our
campfire or smell the smoke."

"We?" She could almost hear the smile in his voice.

"We." Damn you.

Chapter Four

The fire crackled merrily, and oddly enough Danica's new mood nearly matched it. She, or rather they, had made good time today and the bounty hunter felt they could easily catch their prey on the morrow. That fact and the heat in the small hollow they had found left her feeling mellow and at ease. Of course, she knew very well that the best time for relaxation was when chasing down a wanted man or woman; it cleared the mind and sharpened one's wits, leaving a hunter quick to adapt to difficulties. Interestingly, it was time spent between jobs that left her edgy and ill-tempered. She could never think of anything more than the basic needs then, and tended to dwell overmuch on the past.

"Where do you think they're headed?" For a brief time earlier Tucker seemed to think they should sing as they traveled. After she had finally persuaded him there would be no melody forthcoming from either of them, their march together ended in silence. A pity, that, seeing as Danica enjoyed speaking with the lad when he was not acting the fool, or trying to flirt with her. Having said that, even a little flirting would be welcome on the road; any conversation made the time pass more quickly. It seemed her rather heated insistence on a lack of singing offended him, though, and his mouth remained shut until they reached the hollow. Unfortunately the questions started the moment the two travelers stopped, right when she would rather be preparing to rest. After nearly an hour of setting up camp and weathering foolish inquiries like 'Could you teach me the sword?' and 'Why don't you like to sing?', a select few of his endless questions were starting to make sense.

"Chalon De Saudre." The seat of Avoirdupois power, it was the only destination in the West that could be of any use to them. The Rabbit informer's testimony to Delaney only reinforced that fact. It might not make perfect sense to Danica, but it continued to be her only real choice in this direction. It still sticks in my craw; I just can't see the Avoirdupois coming up with this under the circumstances. Have things become that desperate for their Great House? On the other hand, should the worried suspicions she kept to herself prove correct, that particular choice of destination would be logical.

"But why Saudre?" She could see the Raccoon was genuinely perplexed, though for different reasons than she. He knows nearly nothing, Danica. "Why the Avoirdupois? What do the Horselords want with this Grey Fox, anyways? Who is he?"

"These are all questions you should have asked before you followed me, Tucker. You want to be a hunter? Learn." She resolutely ignored his disgusted snort. "Who is he? I have no idea yet." Liar. "What do they want with him? I suppose they want to hand him over to someone in Saudre, someone of importance. Evidently they're convinced a handsome reward awaits them for their troubles; either that or it's a favor for a friend. One in Saudre, or the Fox himself that they're helping out of the city."

"For someone who criticizes my lack of question-asking earlier, you don't seem to have much information yourself," he noted somewhat tartly. A brief silence fell with the Raccoon shifting slightly after a few seconds. It was broken a moment later with yet another query. "A reward or favor? Why do you figure that?"

"Because what's being offered by my employer is fifty aureals. That's not public knowledge, but no doubt the Weasel is aware he's worth some coin." The boy's eyes were now the size of small saucers; the idea of fifty gold aureals was awe-inspiring. Representing well over three years of work for a peasant, it would finance her for considerably less time. When one is forced to move a great deal, costs rise dramatically. Still, it was a comforting sum to be sure, and certainly more coin than Danica had ever seen at one time.

Her good mood was beginning to wilt somewhat under the chain of lies she was forging. Essentially deceiving Tucker about the nature of the group they pursued, she again found herself filled with self-disgust.

"Fifty," he breathed, licking him chops involuntarily "That's, what, nine for Delaney?"

"About seven," she threw back, and he ducked his head in embarrassment. Still not up with his numbers; few were, and just as few could read. Don't taunt him, Danica, she admonished herself sharply, not everyone has the benefit of a formal education.

"Is that usual for a bounty?" Danica looked up at his eager tone, and could see the coins piling up in his head, golden plans for his future unfolding.

This looks all too familiar Just as I thought in the beginning. "This isn't a game, Tucker! Do you know how many people have died for that sort of money, or killed for it? The men, women and children I hunt are criminals, usually desperate and willing to murder to survive. Some have done so well before I get on their trail. Some become quite good at it." She poked the fire moodily. "And yes, before you ask, some of them have been children." This conversation rapidly leeched away her good humor, leaving her frustrated and unhappy. "And no, that's not usual. Most of the time the reward is nearer fifty to a hundred fifty denarii, depending on the crime. Nothing close to this one. You need to keep moving, always switching towns; always chasing after rapists, thieves, and killers." Though she put emphasis on the thieves, Tucker's expression, black mask shadowing his eyes and tail twitching at the tip, told the story: she was not convincing him. "I'm betting you figure on being a justice-bringer, someone who hunts down those who hurt others and take from them," Danica snorted in frustration. "Everyone starts that way, Tuck. Everyone wants to be that way. It never lasts; there's something about hunting people for money that kills the idealism, dries up the conscience...." Her voice trailed off as she noted the blank refusal in his gaze. It infuriated her suddenly, the idea that Tucker thought he, alone among all the others, could be different. Why should he be any better?

"Those knives you keep around, the ones I saw you playing with back at the Crested Mastiff," she said, switching tactics. "You sharpen them after you use them?" He blinked, startled by the seeming change of subject, and nodded warily. "I bet Delaney helped pick them out. Nice, keen edge and point I bet." Again, the nod. "You ever cut someone?"

Suddenly defensive, Tucker produced one, thin and needle sharp for use against light armor. Dexterously he began dancing it along his hands. "Delaney's taught me a fair bit of knife work," he admitted. "Rough and tumble, closing and what to do then. I could probably do fairly well with that heavy bastard you keep at your back," the Raccoon said, flicking a finger at her waist.

"But you haven't used this one, have you?" she concluded. It was obvious he was trying to find a way around that question as well. Finally he shook his head, reluctantly. "Maybe you've pulled it out, waved it in some tough's face, but that's all, right? Knifework's ugly stuff, Tuck. In close and personal, and nobody goes through a knife fight who doesn't walk out cut, win or lose."

"You're not telling me anything I haven't already heard from Delaney ," he replied smugly. "Besides, I'd rather be using something else," he continued, hinting.

With a grunt Danica slipped the sword from its bed in her gear, holding it out to him hilt first. "You think this is better? Take it." When Tucker gripped it, she jerked the sheath away, leaving him holding naked steel. He almost lost the sword then, but recovered, staring at the blade in awe. The firelight shimmered on the steel, transforming razor-edged metal to liquid satin. It shadowed on the oddly shaped runes carved into the base of the blade, and flowed across the howling face formed out of brass on the hilt. If his eyes were wide before, they now grew to truly inspiring proportions. Danica had a brief image of them popping clear out of his head and rolling off the tips of his boots. She stifled a laugh. *He's never even held a sword before, much less one like that. I can see how he might think it's enchanted. I certainly did.*

"It's so light." Tucker twisted it left and right, admiring the play of firelight on the gleaming steel. He peered closely at the hilt and the runes etched into the blade, turning a fascinated eye her way. Danica shrugged.

"It's not actually that light, Tuck, but the balance is very good, and it's not blade heavy like the swords around here. As for the marks, apparently they're the swordmaker's signature. And the name of the sword. As for the face on the hilt, seems that most of the swords from that country have hilts of a similar design; no big guards or anything."

"Named," he whispered. "What is it called?"

Danica shook her head. "My teacher never told me."

Tucker frowned slightly, but only in thought. Danica could see the idea of a mysterious sword kindling a fire in his considerable imagination. *Perfect. Just keep thinking that way, Tuck.* The frown deepened as he examined the blade, though, and the burglar reached for the metal near the hilt. "Blunt?" he whispered, running his finger up the blade. "No, it's-augh!" In embarrassment he jerked the finger back, sucking on it.

"It's razor sharp at the tip, but quite dull at the base. You won't find another like it on Calabria." She shook her head at his unasked question. "I told you no magic, Tuck. Just a different style of sword." Studying him carefully, she prepared to lower the boom. The sword held him rapt as he concentrated on its beautiful craftsmanship. "Looks really nice, right? Feels good in your hand, right?" He nodded enthusiastically, finger still in his mouth, and again Danica would have laughed at his pose were her mood not so serious. "Now, run it through someone's belly. Slip it in, look him in the eyes and watch his face change."

It took a moment for the words to sink in, then Tucker's expression crumbled. He stared at the beautiful piece of metal, now reduced from exotic work of art to killing tool. The moment passed quickly, though. Glancing at her, he stood, holding the sword carefully, and swished it defiantly through the air like an actor in a play.

"I think I could get used to this," Tucker commented, staring directly into Danica's eyes, challenging her.

Bravado. Danica cursed herself silently. Questioning his will to act on his dreamswas the worst thing she could have done. Suddenly it became an issue of a man with something to prove to a woman; after her discussion with Delaney one might think she would have learned. He reached out one hand to her and she slapped the sheath into it, defeated.

"If there's nothing like it anywhere around here, where did you get it?" he asked quietly, fumbling to get the tip of the blade into the simple wooden scabbard.

"My teacher, a fellow I knew a long time ago, before I met you. He came around the Mastiff when I was new there. An albino Leopard; at least, that's what he looked like, but with thicker fur. Mo-gei wasn't much like any person you'd ever meet, though these days if you're lucky you might see his countrymen down near the Docks in Triskellion. He dressed outlandishly, had a bizarre accent, and used that blade. Bounty hunter by necessity, exiled from his own land for some crime he wouldn't talk about - apparently it had to do with family honor. Took me in when I needed it and taught me bits and pieces of the trade. There aren't any schools for this line of work. It's the sort of thing you have to learn through experience." Through survival. The flames were dying; she motioned and he gripped another thick branch, garnered from the meager amount found decorating the floor of the hollow. Little life remained in this campfire. "He taught me how to use a sword his way. It's very different from the fashion here, much like the sword itself. I picked up a fair amount, enough to keep training on my own, before he died."

"Murdered?" whispered Tucker, enraptured with the tale.

She snorted with mixed sadness and loathing. "Killed by a common prostitute. Caught a disease from her. The illness started out like a cold, but it never went away. By the time we realized he was deathly sick, it was too late. Most competent practitioners of Theurgy won't touch bounty hunters. We're tainted; the people we hunt may be criminals, but we do it for money and sometimes kill them." Finally something that hit home solidly. Like most people, Tucker had been raised on songs and stories of the lone bounty hunter, consumed with a need for revenge against the murderers of his teachers. What rot. There had been nothing heroic in Mo-gei's death, only a long, agonized struggle against a terribly patient and uncaring foe. "I watched him slowly fall apart; he went blind, and near the end didn't even know who I was. They talk about it being a mercy when some people die; this was one of those times." Let him stew on that. She drew the sword again while he sat silently and considered her words. "It's late, and I want to be moving before the sun rises. Turn in, Tucker. I have to oil your blood off my blade."

The young burglar eventually got himself settled on the cold, hard ground, wrapping her spare blanket around his long frame. Danica sat and carefully oiled the sword; keep your weapons clean and they can save your life; neglect them and they may fail when you need them most. It was only one of Mo-gei's many teachings. Blood stained metal burned in an imperfection unless oiled away. Enough of them and Mo-gei's legacy would be no more. So Danica sat and oiled, and when she finished wondered about her mentor. Wondered if things might have gone differently between them and Malik, if she could have somehow saved the white Leopard. An old dance; as usual, the hunter found no satisfactory ending. This time, though, she was not the only one kept awake. It was at least a quarter of the night before she heard Tucker's breathing slow to the rhythm of sleep.

Perhaps something did penetrate the young Raccoon's armor of ignorance and idealism after all.

*   *   *

The sky was still full dark when Danica woke. Uncertain what had awakened her, she quickly wrapped fingers around her close-in weapon. First things first. Unmoving save for that initial reflex action, the Fox slowed her breathing despite the frantic beating of her heart and tried to relax her body. Hopefully to a watcher it would seem as though one of the figures under the blankets tensed, perhaps in the grip of a dream, then relaxed again in sleep. Leaving her eyelids slitted, almost fully closed, Danica let other, stronger senses range through the night.

Slowly, circling out from around her and more to the upward side of where she lay, an unseen picture began to form in her mind, painted with sweeps of her ears and nose. First the fire; though she deliberately slept upwind from it, it was close enough that the scent shone out like a beacon, the sharp tang of ashe poplar mixing smoothly with the darker, richer taste of roasted hardwood garnished by Tucker from a farmer's woodpile. Watered and near death, its coals still hissed to her ears clearly, boiling air and seething steadily beneath a thin layer of ash. Near her feet lay Tucker, his breathing light and soft. No snores from this one. Smelling strongly of heavy city food, the sharp sting of cold steel, and his own rather pungent Raccoon aroma, the young thief was a bright spot in the image her senses were forming.

Further out the pattern began to distort, growing longer and thinner due to the confusion of the wind. Upwind from her, from where scent still came clearly, Danica made out the thin, almost undetectable scents of climbing reptiles, out foraging for food in the safety of the night. Her sensitive ears picked out their quiet, nearly inaudible cries to one other. Food here, mate here, my tree. Nothing else, but that was hardly surprising with the breeze blowing in the same direction for the entire night. Only a fool would approach a camp from upwind. But downwind, now that was a different story. Though her nose could catch only the slightest hint, still the faint essence of exotic spices and perfume tickled it for an instant. It might as well be a signature.

Malik.

Leaving or departed already. There was no doubt in Danica's mind that Malik's arrogance had brought him too close to the fire, awakening her, and it was also very likely that he had seen through her improvised deception. The Coyote was extremely clever. Danica cursed softly, hefting the short blade and slipping out of the bedroll to gain a better sense of the situation before the smell faded completely. She glanced at Tucker, but he slept on, oblivious. In the city he's a paranoid Marten, she thought disgustedly, but take him out of reach of the Guard and he drops like a drugged Sloth. Silently she slipped into the thin brush at the edge of the hollow and let her eyes adjust to the deeper shadows, sniffing carefully before moving onward.

The fire, upwind, drowned out most of the odors here, but she definitely captured a trace of Malik's scent. Not long ago at all. Maybe he wakened me by leaving. More disturbingly, perhaps he left after she awoke. With that thought terror swept through the Fox; the other hunter would think nothing of slitting their throats while they slept, for a bounty rich as that offered by the Otter. Worse than that, in his own twisted mind there were plenty of reasons to put a blade in her. Danica cringed, wondering if at that moment he lay somewhere in the darkness, drawing down on her with the crossbow he occasionally used. There would be no warning, nothing seen, nothing heard; just the shock of impact, throwing her to the ground, helpless. Stop it! Desperately she clung to control by clinging to one simple, ugly fact. Had Malik wanted them dead, they would already be so. And there would have been nothing I could have done to stop him. The thought of Tucker and she gasping for a last breath in their bloodied blankets almost made her retch with fear, but the roiling terror in her stomach relaxed after a moment.

She scanned the ground again, letting her eyes dance across the thin grass, broken twigs, and leafy weeds. As the eye wanders, she knew, it picks up a larger picture than one focused on a single spot. This time it latched onto something odd at the same instant her nose caught another, different whiff of scent. Immediately she crouched, staring at the divot left in the ground a few paces away. Certain common signs were obvious to the trained eye and easily identified; a hobnailed boot, turning on the ball of the foot, drove this particular mark into the turf. That's not Malik. Too large, and he doesn't wear boots. Someone came earlier, moved up to look into the hollow, and turned away, creating the gash in the soil. Didn't get too close; not confident in their woodsmanship, or did they just see enough from here? Hopefully the first. She had an uncanny feeling in her spine that this was a mark left by one of those she was pursuing. Mercenaries and soldiers, accustomed to long walks and desiring sure footing during combat, often wore such footgear. Danica suspected she and Tucker were camped far closer to her quarry than she originally thought. The West wind, blowing from their camp to further down the road, became a curse for her. Bending, she sniffed the track as best she could. Not fresh, this track, and

the stink of rust and leather covered most of the smell. The bounty hunter could
not determine what sort of man it had been, if man at all. But you can bet it's
probably not the Wizard, not wearing hobnails.

Turning, Danica surveyed the camp from where the intruder had stood. Tucker
lay close to her, wrapped in his own blankets, with no pack. Still, her leather pack
lay between their bedrolls and that position had been chosen carefully, not by
coincidence. In addition to preventing the thief from rolling closer to her, an
observer would be hard pressed to determine to whom the pack belonged. As for
her armor, the bounty hunter crudely folded the leather and bronze protection
under her pack before she slept, a habit ever since a night lizard had once decided
that the boiled skin of one of its cousins seemed like a good snack. It cost a full
denar to fix the chew marks in the armor, but now she blessed the dratted beast.
You likely saved me here. As for weapons, with her sword slid under her blankets
beside her and the knife under the rolled up cloak she used as a pillow, none of the
usual accouterments of her violent profession were easily visible. So they only know
someone is on the trail behind them, and not the reason why. Quickly moving back
to the camp she resisted the urge to kick Tucker awake. Any danger was long since
gone by now, and the poor Raccoon was exhausted after the day's walk. Fast, agile,
strong...all of these things would describe him quite well. Enduring? Well, that was
another matter. There were few reasons for city folk to develop the proper muscles
and lungs for distance walking.
    Now I just have to figure out if Malik knows where my quarry is. Danica
pondered that question as she fumbled about in her bedroll, beginning the
impossible task of finding the exact, comfortable position she so recently vacated.
Despite the fact the Grey Fox's party was close by, she doubted Malik had discovered
them. Knowing someone else had been lurking around her camp (and a hunter as
experienced as Malik could never miss the marks she discovered) was one thing.
Knowing that he would have to continue downwind from her to find them told
Danica that the Coyote would return to his own bedroll for the night. The
possibility of being caught between two foes would be contrary to his well-developed
survival instincts. He would be watching, though, concealed just out of scent and
hearing. Waiting to determine the best way to remove both her prize and her head.

How Malik caught up with her so quickly was no mystery; obviously he had not
believed a single word she uttered during their conversation. After accepting the
Otter's offer, the Coyote most likely tracked her down at the Crested Mastiff, and
followed at a discreet distance once he determined her travel plans. Perhaps her old
associate even left a half day after her, just in case. As for physically catching up,
Tucker slowed her enough that it would be ridiculously easy for him to make up the
lost time; times past she watched Malik loping along beside her and Mo-gei,
indefatigable, impossibly fresh after the two of them were exhausted. His seemingly
endless endurance had frustrated Mo-gei; it terrified her. Sometimes he seemed less
a man than a magical construct, untiring, unstoppable. Danica did not look
forward to the confrontation she knew was brewing; if not today, then someday

soon. A monster like Malik would never let go of their past. Delaney, where are you when I need you? The brief thought came upon her unawares; she cursed the weakness, reviling herself. The only person Danica could count upon was herself. Besides which, Delaney was in Triskellion. There was no sense praying for help that would never materialize. Rolling over, she took a long look at Tucker then shook her head. The burglar was almost as fast with his hands as she was on her feet, and if Delaney had taught him to use a knife, he knew much more than simple cut and thrust; the old Raccoon was a barrelful of lethal tricks.

Malik would eat the young thief alive.

Heloise, if you're listening to a greedy, tired bounty hunter, please don't let this get Tuck killed. I don't know if I could live with dragging a friend along on this ride to die.

Settling in, Danica resigned herself to an exhausting night. Sleep would prove elusive and fitful.

*　*　*

False dawn, that time of night where the light seems to grow but only tricks the eyes into making shapes out of shadows, was fading when Danica shook Tucker awake. The Raccoon rolled over, his back protesting loudly at the movement, and his watery eyes failing to focus properly on the face silhouetted against the indigo and black sky above. "Wha...?" he whispered, years of avoiding the Guard slapping a gag over his sleep-fuddled instinct to blurt out the question normally. Arrgh. Sleeping on the ground isn't half as fun as you might think. The earth leached away his body heat and left him cold and damp, every joint aching despite his youth.

"Up," the bounty hunter whispered, curtly but to his ears not unkindly. Sniffing as he rolled over, Tucker tasted the scent of her exhaustion hanging in the air. Danica probably lay awake all night, he thought guiltily, guarding the camp while he slept like a newborn. Next time , he vowed, I'll be the one standing watch. It would not be the first time the burglar kept his eyes open the night through; sometimes you needed to watch a house for a long time to get a feel for the holes in its defenses.

"What's going on?" he repeated more clearly if still quietly, swiftly following her example and rolling up his blanket. Watching and learning from her every move certainly gave him enough to think about during this trip. Tucker was beginning to see how much more there was to learn than he first thought. Well, she did say you picked it up as you went along. I can do this, though. When he finished, he tossed the blanket to her; the Red Fox caught it and tied it on the top of her pack. But when the Raccoon started strapping on his knives a hand came down on his wrist. Startled and staring down at her gloved fingers touching his forearm, he almost missed what she said. Not...yet? Why not? Rather than ask questions he placed the sheathed blades back on the ground, pausing to shove one in the back of his belt. There was a lesson Delaney had mercilessly beaten into him; he could still recall the words. Ye might be the best blade artist in the world lad, but it'll do ye nae good if yer knife's left at home. And the time ye'll want it most is the time ye'll nae have it.

This, of course, was after the scarred and (in Tucker's sometime opinion) insane Raccoon burst into his room the morning after a whiskey bender and attacked him with a stick. A painful awakening, it had been.

Quietly Danica led him to the edge of the hollow, moving the last few paces on her knees. He mirrored the bounty hunter, and when she dropped to the ground at the lip, fell down beside her. Slowly extending her arm, the Fox pointed in the direction the sun would rise. At first Tucker could see nothing across the grey and black plain, but then a flicker of light caught his eye. There, across the shadowy expanse of fields, flickered a small fire. He squinted and could just keep it in focus, occasionally able to discern a dark form slipping around the flames. Straining his eyes earned him nothing more; the thief was forced to give up. In the gloom of pre-dawn, the other camp was too indistinct for details to be observed. Another quiet tap on his wrist drew him back to the campsite. "Was that them?" he whispered as they crouched beside the stone-cold ashes.

Danica nodded thoughtfully. "We made up a lot of time on them, but I can't imagine how. Unless they've been dawdling, we should be farther behind. It's a problem; one of them came around the camp last night for a sniff."

"What!" Tucker managed to contain the explosion at the last second; as a result, it gurgled out as a rather strangled exclamation. "When? How do you know?"

"I don't know when, Tuck, but it was after I went to sleep. So make it the middle of the bloody night," she replied irritably. "How do I know? I woke up and found some tracks. The good news, if there is any, is that I don't think he would have figured us for anything more than travelers who left a little late and got caught on the road at sundown."

"I'd say that sounds good," Tucker started warily, "but something tells me there's more bad coming."

"You might want to take up a career as a fortune-teller, Tuck," Danica sighed, kicking dirt over the already dead coals. Staring down at her feet she seemed to come to a decision, and swung to face him. "We have a very, very big problem. There's an ex-partner of my mentor wandering around out here. I think he knows about this job, he knows we have a lead, and he's following us to take it away." She sat down on one of the logs and slumped over, head in gloves.

Tucker stared at her, shocked. Another bounty hunter she knew? Why was her reaction so extreme? Never once had he seen her this despondent. Angry, yes. Furious even. Sad and, he was convinced, desperately lonely. But this, this broken depression was completely stupefying. Frightening as well. Tentatively, he reached out for her shoulder but then, thinking better of it, drew his hand back equally slowly. Something quietly whispered in the Raccoon's ear that to touch her now would not leave her looking kindly upon him, and for once he listened. The burglar watched her ears twitch at the faint rustle of a scavenging lizard in the tree above, and he frowned in consternation as she tensed reflexively.

Fear. There was fear there, too.

"Danica," he whispered, sitting down on the log beside her. Not too close, now.

"Who is this man? You have to tell me."

"Malik," she returned. "His name is Malik. He might look like a Coyote, but he's a serpent. Cold, vicious, and uncaring. Poisonous. He's been a hunter as long as I've known him, and for a lot longer before that. Mo-gei, my mentor, worked together with Malik some of the time. In a bizarre way they were friends, good friends. I never personally understood how you could get to be friends with a maddened cobra. For my part, Malik was certainly never any more than someone to be feared."

Tucker shifted uncomfortably; this was a completely new side to Danica. Always the hard surface, always the sharp edge, never showing emotions. He knew there was something deeper, but now that it had surfaced the thief was stunned by the raw dread she displayed. Keep listening? That seemed wisest. She must be really shaken to be telling me this.

"For a long time the three of us worked together, Mo-gei, myself, and sometimes Malik." She smiled thinly. "Sort of a family, I suppose, with a father, a daughter, and a vagrant older son. Seeing I was a bit of an orphan, for want of a better term, I can't say I minded much having a few people around to look out for me, even if Malik kept a bad feeling running up and down my spine." Tucker's ears perked up at this; though Delaney knew of Danica's past the innkeeper was not terribly forthcoming. The young burglar never understood that way of thinking. If you knew something critical about a friend, was it not just as important to share it with her other friends, in order for them to understand her better?

"The last time he worked with us, we were on a hunt for two youngsters. It was a particularly horrible crime. They'd been servants to a Bisclavret household and butchered the noble lady, running off with her valuables. The three of us tracked them for days. We almost lost them quite a few times, but Mo-gei was very insistent." For an instant a ghost of a smile touched her lips. "His number one rule was that if you take on a job, you get it done. No excuses. "So Malik, he put forth an effort like you've never seen. I always knew that Coyote tracked like a demon, but this? He hunted those murderers through heavy forest, swamps, rivers; it was unbelievable. And he did it all for Mo-gei; for once both he and I agreed on letting them go, just for different reasons. Me because I was feeling sorry for them, and Malik because he simply couldn't be bothered." Danica swallowed hard and glanced at him out of the corner of her eye. Another surprise. In anyone else Tucker would have read it as guilt, but Danica never, ever looked guilty. "So we did catch them, after almost a week of serious hunting. Two children - a girl and her brother, both of them no older than ten or eleven." She shook her head, a disgusted frown twisting her mouth. "Servants? They were slaves."

Tucker sucked in a breath. Slavery was an unpleasant fact on Calabria, and nowhere more prevalent than the lands of Great House Bisclavret, its practice sanctioned by the laws of the rulers. His sister, Seanna, spoke often at great length against slavery, and after listening to a few escaped slaves, hearing how they were treated, Tucker decided long ago nothing good could come of it. After all, the young thief would never wish to be a slave. How could he condone it for someone else? And for children, yet....

"I got their stories out of them," Danica continued, tone light and almost bland. The fur around her eyes rippled as the skin tightened, and Tucker smelled the rage. "Bisclavret slaves are treated pretty poorly, by and large, worse in general than in most other lands. Slavery's lawful there, even encouraged, right? So you can't get arrested for breaking your own property." Her smile, like her logic, was ugly. "The sister stuck a pitchfork in the back of the noble lady while she was horsewhipping the girl's brother for stealing a dessert from the kitchen. Seems the countess liked to dish out punishment to her slaves personally. They took her valuables and ran. Seeing as the lady's estate was on the edge of Bisclavret territory, it was easy for them to evade the Guard, so bounty hunters were summoned. The children even told us our employer, the lady's husband, made his money in the slave trade." For the first time Danica looked Tucker in the eyes. "This rather disturbed Mo-gei, and had me nearly raving. But Malik, he was fine with it."

She rose suddenly and began to pace, arms beginning to sweep the air as she grew more disturbed. Tucker could see her eyes take on a faraway cast as the memories drew her back to that time. "So Mo-gei, going with his ethic of always completing any contract agreed to, starts back with the children. I'm not happy, so I keep telling him we have to let the children go. Malik and I get into an enormous argument and Mo-gei starts becoming very edgy, like I've never seen before. Malik doesn't miss it, and stops arguing with me, but it's too late. Mo-gei's already starting to question the whole thing, to question himself. Why, he asks, are we taking children back to their deathscertain death?" She stopped suddenly and looked back towards the town, eyes scanning the horizon. Shocked, Tucker realized Danica was looking for her erstwhile associate; the telling of the story obviously brought her concerns about him to the forefront.

"So I wake up that night with a bad feeling, only to find Malik and the children gone. I hear movement close by but heading off, and realize that if I take the time to wake up Mo-gei, I'll lose them. So I hop up and take off after the sound, following the trail - three people." Danica shot a glance at Tucker; he nodded, anxious for her to continue. "I'm gaining, but slowly. I come to the edge of the swamp, and there's Malik with the two children. I'm close enough to hear them speak. He tells them he's had enough and says that if they take off across this swamp, he'll lead the pursuit off another way. They're wary, but he tells them he'll give them a bit of coin to get out of his life. He reaches around behind his back, as if to bring out a purse. But I see him take out the knife." Another quick look at him, and the burglar pretended not to see it. In truth, he found the tale very disturbing, and could hardly blame Danica for her insecurities. "He grabs the girl by the snout and cuts the boy's throat, shoving him under the water. A heartbeat later and she's down too." Tucker's eyes widened as his heart lurched.

"But why didn't you-"

"Dammit Tuck! Don't you think I haven't asked myself that?" Danica shook her head. "I really, really didn't expect him to do that. And he did it so cursed quickly, I couldn't react in time. Then, by the time he went for the girl, I froze. I just-" She made a quick gesture in the air. It could have meant anything. "I've seen men gutted and women torn apart, Tuck. It's never easy to watch a person die. And I've watched Malik gut some of those men, and women too. I'd killed a few myself. But that? It was too much. Not even my brother...." She paused, and shifted her shoulders around, trying to work out some of the tension. Shuddering, Tucker tried to imagine what she felt that night, then immediately attempted to banish it from his mind. It was no use; the image remained locked in his mind's eye. And Danica was continuing, as unable to stop speaking as he was to stop listening. With the worst over, so he thought, she was a bit calmer now. "I slipped back, as quietly as I could. I don't want to think about what would have happened if he had seen me; I'd probably have joined the children. Then I ran. I ran back to the camp as quickly as I could and told Mo-gei. He very nearly didn't believe me." She slowly sat back down on the log beside the thief. "Malik came back and started in with some story about how he'd lost them off in the marshes, gesturing off in a slightly different direction. He offered to take us there so we could all have a look around, knowing full well he was the best tracker. But Malik's weak point is his ego; he forgot I'm no slouch as a tracker myself. It's part of being a Fox. And when I pointed out the actual trail to Mo-gei, there was nothing he could say. That's when Mo-gei finally decided I'd been telling the truth."

"What happened?" Tucker whispered, still caught up in the horror.

"They fought. Oh, with words, not weapons. Malik practically pleaded with Mo-gei to understand. He thought he was doing the right thing. He would have told Mo-gei and me that they'd escaped, led us around in circles away from the bodies, and come back later for their slave tattoos. He could see Mo-gei had been caught between dedication to the job and his own compassion and sense of ethics. So Malik explained he was just getting the job done, and taking away Mo-gei's suffering by bringing it onto himself." The twisted smile was back on her face. "It was a poor argument, and Mo-gei saw right through it. Greed and madness, that's all there was to what Malik did."

Abruptly Danica spat, as if clearing a bad taste from her mouth. Tucker did nothing but stare at the ground; this sort of thing was far outside of his experience. He knew of some monsters in the city, but none like this ever crossed his path before. The Fox's voice was dull when she began to speak again. "Mo-gei and I abandoned him; I wanted us to kill him, but Mo-gei wouldn't go along with it. He told me later that Malik had saved his life years before. After that, I watched my teacher age in front of me, as if that final revelation about his friend was too much for his spirit. He started drinking and whoring. A bit over a year later he died." Flat as paper now, her tone told Tucker she had finished the tale. The important part, anyway. "And now Malik's out there. He was only a few paces from us last night." The thought put a dagger of ice into Tucker's gut; he sucked in a breath, trying desperately not to give in to the quick and brutal impulse to look over his shoulder.

"Um, Danica," he began quietly. She certainly would not take this well. "Why don't...I mean, you always told me it wasn't worth dying for gold. Why don't we just, you know, go back to the inn?"

Hands instantly grabbed his shoulders, jolting his head up. Her wild eyes stared into his, her nose so close he could taste her breath. A position he had dreamed of, with distressing frequency, but not in this way. "No! I'm not walking away from a contract! I took it, made a promise, Tuck! You don't walk away from a job! It's your life if you do!" She released him and slid back, staring at her gloved hands. "I can't walk away from this one," she whispered, more to herself than to him.

What in the name of the Light is going on here? Tucker had his own suspicions about the Grey Fox, but could not for the life of him discern the motive for Danica's frantic insistence to forge on. She's a friend. You support your friends, even when you don't understand them. "Fine," he breathed out, then more loudly. "Fine. We'll do this. There's two of us, and one of him, Danica. If we can deal with the Wizard and her white-shields, we can deal with this bounty hunter of yours."

Her head snapped up and the fiery glare almost tumbled him from the log. "You stay away from him, Tucker! Do you understand? He'll kill you with the same effort it takes you to step on a beetle." Her voice rose higher in pitch, almost frantic, and Tucker made quick shushing motions. "You haven't a clue what you're dealing with here. I'd give Delaney good odds, but you? You've never killed a man. He'd gut you in a second!" A sharp retort sprang to mind, but the naked terror in her eyes shocked him into silence. Her words cut but their driving force mollified him. The Red Fox cared for him, at least a little; a soothing balm for injured pride. He settled on giving her a stiff nod. Relieved, she relaxed somewhat. Well, as much as she ever does.

"C'mon, Tuck," she said awkwardly, obviously embarrassed at her emotional outbursts. "It's almost dawn. Let's finish up here and have a look at who we're up against."

Chapter Five

While they finished packing up the camp, Danica repeatedly attempted to drive home the point to Tucker that he would not receive any share of the bounty. In addition, should trouble occur, as it likely would, he had best stay far out of her way. As a last ditch struggle at keeping the burglar from continuing, it sorely lacked any punch. She sincerely doubted her words made any impression at all on the young thief.

In the odd light before the sun rose she made out her prey for the first time, haloed against the brightening horizon.

"Stay low when you move," she hissed at Tucker, though they were still at a considerable distance away. The burglar glared at her in annoyance. Slipping out of the small grove he kept his silence far better than she, despite lack of familiarity with the rural terrain. She studied her quarry's camp. Perhaps 'a considerable distance away' was a truer measure of the distance reckoned against the amount of time it would take to walk between the two fires than it was in terms of how far they already traveled. They were ridiculously close, really. Had they pressed on a bit longer the night before, she and Tucker would have stumbled right over their quarry in the dark. And wouldn't that have been a pretty picture. The wind must have carried the scent of their campfire directly to the Wizard and her companions, explaining their midnight visitor. So it was definitely them, rather than some hireling of Malik's. The Coyote worked alone most of the time; anyone who could stand to work with him more than once usually tried to kill him for the reward money. Obviously no one had yet succeeded, and Danica did not hold out much hope of that fortuitous event occurring.

Studying her targets from behind one of the trees surrounding the hollow, the bounty hunter tracked each of their movements and tried to make some sense of them. Tucker wormed a few paces closer to slide up under a bush.

Five of them, one standing motionless in the dim light, so still she almost missed the silhouette, and four scattered hither and thither. As her eyes adjusted to the distance Danica could make out three of them chasing the fourth, running him down despite his frantic bursts of speed, slowly boxing him in. She observed his movements, his methods of attempting to escape, and recognized them as similar to her own when pursued. Instinct was a powerful tool and easily identified by race. It seemed the Grey Fox was not with the others by choice. Danica shook her head, fighting against renewed doubt and suspicion. Determinedly, she put aside her concerns and worries over the identity of the Fox, and tried to focus only on studying her competitors, for want of a better word.

One of the pursuers was tall, powerfully built, and very quick, easily closing distance on the Fox but having difficulty on the turns. From the height and movement, she suspected it was a Tiger. *I hope it isn't Salamin the slave trader. That would be the icing on this cake.* Rumor, confirmed by Delaney, described Salamin as an Atavist, a baresark who had attained the ability to submerge his mind into instinct during combat, losing much of his intellect but gaining terrible powers of the body as a result. If he were one of the mercenaries, she could be in very deep trouble. But that doesn't make sense. Salamin is a slaver, his own master, and makes fine money selling to the Bisclavret or foreigners. Why would he demote himself to a simple guard? As for the other two, judging by the easy coordination they displayed in running down their quarry, she guessed they were Bisclavret mercenaries. Wolves, and probably pretty happy to be heading into Avoirdupois lands rather than those of the Doloreaux. The Wolves and the Boars held nothing in common save a shared border and mutual hatred.

As she watched, one of them sprung through the air, catching hold of the desperate Fox with a hand and bringing him down. The huge figure arrived an instant later, and slammed a foot down on the captive until the other two had him under control. Danica turned her gaze towards the fire when it became apparent the chasers had no intention of actually harming her prize. The figure standing by the flames, heavily cloaked, merely observed as the mercenaries dragged the Fox back to the camp. The Fire Wizard. The captive whipped his body about like a Weasel, but try as he might could not escape the Tiger's grasp. A sick feeling crept over Danica as she watched him fighting to get free - his unceasing, tireless attempts seemed almost preternatural in their tenacity. When the three white-shields returned to the camp carrying the struggling fox, they clustered in a circle, no doubt tying him with cord. The cloaked figure turned back to the small cooking fire and began toying with the pot hanging over the coals.

Danica picked up a small pebble and threw it into Tucker's bush. He started, then rolled to look at her. A slow movement of her arm motioned him back, and he slid over the ground like butter in a hot pan, without any of the noise. They both tumbled back into the hollow, Tucker's eyes again wide with excitement, Danica's narrow as she planned quickly and carefully. I have to get him out of there. The disquiet at her core intensified as she considered the Grey Fox in the hands of the Wizard. If he was who she suspected....

But how to free him? They could not just walk up and take him. Though the very idea enjoyed a certain appeal, the bounty-hunter knew that bravado aside, her chances against three sellswords and a Wizard were next to none if they saw her coming. We need to get past them, lay an ambush. The question was how to do that without taking too much time. Avoirdupois lands were close ahead, a half day's march at the most, and within the next hour, they would likely be encountering Rinaldi border patrols. Out of the corner of her eye the hunter caught a glimpse of Tucker opening his mouth, then closing it carefully. Apparently the Raccoon now thought before speaking, a useful skill to master. Still, it might be wise to hear what he had to say; there were no such things as poor ideas, just ideas that could not possibly work given the particular circumstances....

Wait a minute. Tucker?

The plan exploded in her head full-born - audacious, wild, and requiring little effort. Best of all, it was simple. Quickly Danica began to pack her armor; leather with steel and bronze plates, it took much less time to stuff into a backpack than the heavier sort. Nimble feet were her main asset when trouble broke out and the armor barely slowed her when she wore it. Now, however, it would serve her better hidden, until they passed her quarry. "Tucker," she hissed, "if you are coming, snag that gear and wrap it in your blanket like a peasant pack." A pause. "You do know how to roll something up in a blanket to carry it, don't you?"

"I'll be coming with you." His mouth was set, his eyes determined. As expected. If anything, her little fumble last night seemed to have ignited the smoldering flame of his wish to begin the adventurous and prosperous life of a bounty hunter. Then the fire faded momentarily, and the Raccoon opened his mouth in a wide, happy grin that stabbed her conscience deeply. "But you're going to have to help me pack this; I've never had to move anything around before, eh?"

He's totally clueless, and here I am, dragging him into this... "You...," words failed her for an instant, and she lashed out, catching his coat. The Raccoon's dark eyes opened wide as she prepared to lace into him. "If you foul this up for me, if you make a mistake here..." if you get killed "...I'm going to be very, very unhappy with you," Danica finished lamely, suddenly shaken by the realization of the danger facing the young thief. Heloise, I can't lose him! Tucker and Delaney, along with Desmond and Porter, comprised her entire, terribly small circle of friends. For any one of them to die, or disappear from her life, she realized, would be a terrible blow. And here was Tuck, about to walk into a situation rife with lethal possibility, and he was doing it for her.

He nodded somberly, perhaps finally grasping the seriousness of the matter. "Looks to me like our friend the Fox isn't exactly going to be helping them if something goes awry." She nodded tersely. Oddly enough, he didn't appear surprised, almost as though he expected it. "What's the plan?" So earnest now. And yet, there was a hint of that hilarity peeping out from behind the mask. Danica suddenly realized he would never know just what the world was really like until it reared up and savagely bit him. Such naivete, such idealism, was strange to find in a burglar. It was quite a surprise for her to also discover she liked him far better as he was. Better as he is now than as I am. Perhaps Tucker was a small lifeline to a brighter outlook. She took a deep breath and let it out, trying to smile. For him, for everything he did for her. A little smile... he deserves that much.

"Plan? We walk right by. Simple as that."

*   *   *

On the surface it seemed a preposterous idea. Was there possibly a better way to call attention to themselves? Tucker very briefly argued that point before she explained her plan. There was no reason for the Wizard and her sellswords to suspect any skullduggery; Tucker and Danica would be simply two more travelers on the East Road. The group ahead already knew someone followed them on the road and probably had a very good idea what they looked like based on the previous night's reconnaissance. Though it was possible the Wizard would be anticipating pursuers, why these particular two travelers, making no attempt to conceal themselves? Anyone could be moving along the East Road; it was the main trade route between Triskellion and the Avoirdupois. More likely the small group of kidnappers was paying more careful attention to the surrounding countryside, watching for ambushes, than examining every man, woman, and child on the route.

Unfortunately there remained a single, major complication with the plan: in order to pass their quarry this early in the morning, Danica and Tucker would have started out on their traveling very early. Far earlier, in fact, than normal for the average traveler between towns. While not exactly waving banners and bugling, it might attract unwanted suspicion.

With that in mind, Danica decided a bit of banner waving and bugling would be perfect.

"...and furthermore, you're a bloody fool if you think this life would suit you. It's hard work, you know; the sort of thing you aren't used to. Living on the road..."

The revised plan called for the bounty hunter and burglar to argue as they marched past the Wizard's camp. With people on the road too far to be properly heard by anything but a particularly long-eared bat, Danica and Tucker would nevertheless present the image of a pair of quarreling travelers. It was an image she fervently hoped would stick in the minds of the watchers, allowing them to pass without suspicion. Far better to call attention to one detail than try to hide everything and fail. As long as the pair avoided overacting, the Wizard and her guards would be tricked into seeing a completely different image than the truth.

Unfortunately, though the argument started out as a bit of a joke, soon Danica and Tucker found themselves at a loss for amusing subjects. After all, one could only fight about Delaney's odd personal habits for so long. Besides which, Tucker's depiction of the Innkeeper's interesting knife-training sessions had the hunter fighting to hold in peals of laughter. Searching for ideas, Danica decided it would be a good time to force Tucker to listen to some hard truths about her profession. He was, as it were, a captive audience.   It was possible she put forth her arguments a trifle more harshly than necessary.

"...you weren't so bloody boarheaded, you'd see that if I'm not a Prince of the Auvoirdupois, I'm not a Phelan savage either. If spending a little time with me is a chore, well..."

Tucker, for his part, obviously deemed it a fine occasion to bring his long simmering attraction for her out into the open and promptly did so. In short order it became obvious he'd held back a good bit of frustration when dealing with her under normal circumstances. Catching the tone of real passion into his voice, Danica began to suspect his feelings for her had progressed beyond a simple crush. Abruptly she felt herself becoming snappish, wanting only for him to drop the subject.

Since neither party agreed with any part of the other's point, the 'discussion' went rapidly downhill. Despite her anger, Danica suddenly became acutely aware that their rising voices skirted dangerously close to the boundary of overdoing the act. Ironic, to be truthful, for the argument had shifted from staged to real long before they'd drawn near the other group. Maybe they'll think we're a couple, traveling, she thought despairingly, adjusting her pack, rather than a couple of travelers. A quick glance at the camp as they passed told the story. The Wizard's back was to the road, the woman ignoring them, and while the mercenaries certainly showed interest, paying them quite a bit of attention, it was not interest of a dangerous sort. From the road she could see handshaking going on between the two wolves. Wagering, no doubt, on the chances of the travelers' argument leading to blows. Definitely a Tiger, and not Salamin, she noted, in a corner of her mind, while trying to cut in over Tucker's rising voice. The huge whiteshield turned away from them, evidently losing interest, and strode to a squirming bundle on the ground. For an instant an icy chill ran through Danica, and she stumbled over a point designed to reduce Tucker to a quivering, agreeable lump. The Fox. So very close, and so many answers there, some of which she would probably be very happy never knowing. Tucker's voice brought her rudely back to the present.

"...not even listening to me, and that's bloody typical too! I'm not a boy, you know; I've been around for a while, and could probably teach you a few things about life myself."

Yes, how to live it wearing blinders, how to see only the good, how to stumble through it through sheer luck. It was truly a shame she considered sadly, while firing a blistering salvo of oaths in the burglar's face, that she was not the slightest bit interested in the young Raccoon the way he wished. Everything he was saying was absolutely correct. She could do much worse in a man than Tucker. But he was an annoying younger brother to her and could, quite honestly, do much better in a woman. Danica was definitely not interested, for his own good as well as her own.

Was she saddened a bit by the thought? Perhaps. But only a bit.

They came to a small dip in the road, enough to be shielded them from any prying eyes behind them. From this point, the East Road sloped gently downhill straight into Horselands. Danica looked ahead, scanning the horizon for Rinaldi outrider patrols; they would be mounted, most likely, and easy to see with the sun behind her. "Enough, Tuck. We're far enough away that they can't hear us any more."

"...an insult, did you know? A bloody insult that you keep...""Tuck!"

There was a pause in his diatribe, and Tucker blinked owlishly. "Ah, yes. Sorry." Abruptly every word he spat out during their little tiff seemed to come crashing down on him, and his scent rapidly shifted from anger to embarrassment. The young burglar began laughing, slightly hysterically, and scratching frantically at the back of his neck. "Dani, I, that is..."

"Save it. We haven't much time." Danica expected him to be hurt; instead he looked relieved. I'll never understand men. Never. "There isn't much distance left to Avoirdupois lands; we'll be hitting Rinaldi outrider patrols soon enough. So we'll take them here." With a flick of her wrist she indicated the countryside, notably devoid of convenient cover. "Catching them off guard is absolutely crucial. The two of us can't handle a Wizard and three of her men when they're wary." The hunter paused, squinting up at him appraisingly as she unwrapped her sword from the side of her pack. "How good are you at looking worried?"

"In the face of imminent death, I'm a bloody thespian," he joked.

"Good. Because that's precisely what you'll be up against if you aren't convincing." Standing up, Danica pointed the sheathed blade at his chest. "Tuck, one more thing. This is your last chance to get out." He cocked a skeptical eyebrow, and she promptly poked him in the breastbone. "Seriously, Tuck. If you stick around to help me here, you're certainly going to have to fight. You might even have to kill someone." Muscles in her jaw clenched. "You might get hurt, yourself."

There was that smile again, oh so confident and so completely ignorant of reality. "You think I'll walk now? No fear there." The Raccoon made a quick show of checking two of his knives. Forcing her fists to unclench, Danica lowered the sword and returned to her pack. She'd done her best. It was his choice now.

So why did she still feel responsible?

Another thought, spurred by his earlier words, jumped into her head and the bountyhunter looked back over her shoulder. "Oh, and Tuck?" The Raccoon looked up again, eyes narrowing and lips tightening. She smiled, baring all of her teeth. "Don't call me Dani."

*   *   *

Tucker squeezed her arm, the signal that their targets were within sight. Some of the water he was pouring into her mouth ran down her neck and into her fur as his attention lapsed. The Fox bit back a growl, changing it into a cough. At this distance, a sharp-eared Wolf might be able to make out whispers, not the full content, but enough to put him on his guard. The picture they wished to present was hardly one of two people having a quiet conversation. Hence the groaning, and Tucker's muttered expletives as he examined her leg. Danica felt she should definitely have words with him when this was over; though not quite too familiar, he still carried the examination a trifle beyond what was required for the deception. *If I can still speak when this is over.*

"Sirs! Sirs!" Tucker leapt from his crouch and began waving enthusiastically at the travelers. They were watching, Danica noted. Studying the group through slitted eyes, she was careful to use only her peripheral vision to observe. People, she discovered in the past, could often sense direct observation; it was something that created considerable difficulty when stalking a target. The Wizard motioned to the two Wolves; they split up, moving away from their employer, the Tiger hefting the captive Fox effortlessly over his shoulder. *Make or break here,* Danica thought, watching them carefully. One of the lupine sellswords moved closer, while the other took up a flanking position, studying the terrain for possible ambushes and hopefully realizing not even a Stoat would be able to creep within a stone's throw without being seen. Neither of them readied bows or crossbows nor appeared even to carry them; a sudden, incongruous pang of relief struck the bounty hunter. Despite the fact this little drama was only beginning, she felt a surge of confidence run through her veins.

"Speak, 'coon!" The Wolf's sword remained in its scabbard, but his hand rested on the hilt and he shifted a shield to arm. Danica noted the chain armor; though not the most expensive of protection, it was in very good repair and while in the style of Great House Bisclavret's soldiers, it lacked the family markings. Mercenaries, possibly down on their luck, but meticulous in the maintenance of their hauberks which were finely polished and oiled. Too many soldiers let their discipline go lax after mustering out, to their painful dismay the first time poorly cared for arms or armor failed them in desperate circumstances.

"My wife...she's been struck by a red-bander! We just stopped for a quick meal, and the snake came out and bit her on the ankle...."

Danica could imagine what they were thinking as Tuck continued to ramble hysterically. The two travelers from the camp behind them getting a very early start, hoping to put in a good few miles before breakfast. An argument, and the decision to stop for a bit of food to cool down, talk out their differences. And now they sat in the midst of a scattering of food and packs, one frantic, the other lying still, wrapped up in a cloak against the cool morning air. The Bisclavret mercenary nodded and sprinted back to the Wizard and her hulking bodyguard, his explanation accompanied by wide sweeps of arms. The other Wolf remained watching; Danica observed his nose working frantically as he tried to make sense of the situation, searching for any hint of duplicity. We're not downwind, so it won't be easy for him to make anything out, and the spiced meat all over the place should mess up his nose a little. Enough, hopefully, for him to miss the sharp tang of metal in the air. She saw the Weasel shake her head in negation under the hood of the cloak, the Tiger turning away to stare down the road. The whiteshield nodded slowly, face grim, and turned back.

"We can pay!" Tucker held out his purse, opening it up and taking out a handful of denarii, amongst which glittered a scattering of gold. Danica blessed the young burglar's timing. The nearer Wolf sucked in his breath at the sight. When I count that, there better be four aureals or Tuck's going to have some explaining to do. Many people never laid eyes on gold, and mercenaries were no exception, save when very lucky during looting. It often proved to be an irresistible lure, undermining common sense and natural caution.

And morals, a little voice inside noted. How much of the Otter's words do you really believe, Danica?

"They've a fair bit o'money, even some gold," the mercenary called back to his associates, his speech marked by the heavy Bisclavret accent so similar to Delany's. "Where'd ye get it from?" he inquired, turning back and shouting across the distance.

"We're moving to Saudre," yelled Tucker, almost hopping now. "Got a good price for the house. I'm not looking for someone to take her there, man! Just to the nearest town where we might find a healer. I don't want to wait for a patrol; she might die by then! Truth and Beauty, she's dying now, dammit!"

The Weasel tugged at the first Wolf's arm, whispering something. He nodded and grinned, obviously relieved, and perhaps for more than the money. Then the entire group, including the Tiger carrying the helpless captive, began to move closer.

"Why don't we just have some fun?" she heard the big cat rumble, heedless of the volume of his voice. "There's a woman and gold; we could take both from this little ratspit. Who cares if she's dying?" Danica wrinkled her lip in disgust and felt Tucker tense beside her. Definitely can't lose this little tussle.

The Wizard shot a venomous glace at him from under her heavy leather hood; somehow the mercenary missed it. The first Wolf was not so circumspect and rounded on the massive warrior, fur bristling and hand on the hilt of his sword. "I do what I'm paid to do, and there's a limit fer that too. If ye be wanting to rob and terrorize, take yerself elsewhere." The Tiger spat angrily, but the Wolf was not impressed. He leaned in closer, nearly muzzle to muzzle with the huge feline, completely unafraid. "Or me brother and I might be willing to pin ye to a tree and show ye how we deal with yer like up North, stripey. D'ye ken what a blood eagle is?"

The growl started low, a deep rumble in the Tiger's chest that Danica imagined she could feel in hers, but the Wizard pushed between the two before it rose to its peak, a savage attack cough. The whip-thin, hooded figure faced the huge, armored behemoth, whispering angrily. Even with her sharp Fox's hearing Danica only made out a few words. Something to do with everburning flame? And his liver? It was enough; the Tiger's ears fell back, and on the wind Danica caught a sudden whiff of his fear. He nodded, angrily striking the Fox when the Wizard turned away. Another one I owe you, Danica noted angrily. His burden kicked out once in protest then wisely lay still.

The Weasel moved closer, perfunctorily motioning Tucker away. He stepped back a few paces, bowing hastily and clumsily; the silent Wolf came to stand beside him, still sniffing cautiously. Danica groaned; she hoped it sounded more real to them than it did to her. Certainly some of it was unfeigned, with her sword beneath her, hilt digging painfully into her back. "Let me see that leg," whispered the Wizard, reaching out with thin, fine-boned hands. When her fingers touched the cloak, the Weasel gasped, no doubt feeling hardened leather and greaves of metal beneath the swaddling.

Danica lashed out, one hand gripping the Wizard by her formidably thick cloak, the other hammering a fist-sized stone between her eyes. The woman staggered, somehow keeping her feet, dragging the bounty hunter over. A ragged burst of an ancient language brought flickers of bright crimson flame to gather instantly about one hand, while she foolishly fumbled with a heavy mace at her belt. Danica struck again, the blow solid under the Weasel's jaw, felling her, leaving a thin trail of crimson whipping through the air behind the falling body. One! Shouts exploded as the bounty hunter spiraled to her feet, snatching her sword on the way up and discarding the scabbard. In an instant she knew the plan had changed for the worse.

Originally they hoped to take the Wizard hostage, should she be the first to examine Danica. If not, and the Weasel not in easy reach, it would have been a good time to flee and try something else later. With the mercenaries lacking any ranged weapons, and the Wizard likely not wanting to expend her magic against already fleeing 'bandits', Danica felt the plan was without much risk.

Up until this point, everything could not have proceeded better, but the now supine Wizard had failed to fall on the first blow and the Wolves reacted much more quickly than expected. One was pulling steel and closing far too swiftly to think about holding a blade to the Weasel's throat. The other grappled with Tucker on the ground nearby. Either the boy had leapt on him the moment Danica struck the Weasel, or the Wolf had disdained drawing his sword; whatever the reason, the two were locked in a vicious struggle, teeth and claws flashing as they sought a hold. It seemed a close match, the mercenary's chain armor advantage countered by the shield weighing down his left arm. With Delaney as a teacher, Tucker ought to know what he's doing infighting. He'd better not hesitate going for the throat. It was the only thought she had time for before the second Wolf was on her.

Danica avoided a blow from his sword with a quick skip to the side, disdaining contact. The mercenary recovered and stabbed out, shield covering his left, staying cautious. Sliding off line, Danica cut his sword hand and sawed down his wrist to thrust deeply into his right shoulder, chain mail links parting under her weight behind the thin, razor sharp blade. Her victim let out a shrill cry, dropping his weapon and falling back, trying to shake loose the shield from his other arm as blood pumped from the deep wound. Two! She let him go, spinning to face the Tiger, continuing the spin to avoid his massive axe. The double-bladed weapon sliced the air where she had stood a mere heartbeat before, and Danica faced him with barely two paces separating them.

The big mercenary grinned lazily. She recognized the look in his golden eyes; having decided its prey was weak, a cat was in the mood to play. *He may be right; a lot more speed there than he has any right to, and I can't block that kind of power. Thank Heloise I took care of the other one so quickly. Just like Mo-gei always said...put them down fast; one at a time is much better than two at once.* Danica spared a glance for Tucker. He was on top of the Wolf, and was pressing his weight down on the dagger between them; she could see it was one of his own. A faint sound warned her; even the brief distraction was nearly too much, and once again her only saving grace were nimble feet. This time the moon-shaped blade came so close it nearly shaved off one of her ears. The Tiger laughed, a long, roaring bellow, and the Fox took the opportunity to flick the tip of her blade at his eyes. With a sharp snarl he swung his axe against her sword, leaping back with tail lashing. "I was going to have a bit of fun with you," he rumbled, "but now I think I'll just hack you in two."

Danica said nothing, balanced evenly on the soles of her feet. The striped monster leaped forward, axe blurring through an X before him. Danica gave ground, then sideslipped; he could charge much swifter than she could backpedal. To continue to retreat was suicide. Again her blade licked out; this time the hunter aimed lower, and the razor tip of the sword cut through a boot, gashing his calf. His

grunt of effort turned into a yelp of pain and the axe came around one handed in a powerful, looping backhand. She dropped straight down to avoid it, rolling away quickly to regain good footing as the double-blade hissed by above, left hand twitching the fold of her cloak around her. Limping, but not seriously impaired, the Tiger closed relentlessly. "Your cloak is a poor shield, little girl, no matter what you've been taught. Let me...demonstrate." This time he came in more carefully, his patterns tighter. The heavy axe swept out, back, and up in short, powerful arcs, any of which could easily cut through her leather and metal armor. The Tiger's chain shirt, reaching down to the lower belly and covering his upper arms, was adequate protection against Danica's blade. But his movements left openings; she cut his left wrist, and struck from there at his face. A fraction too slowly; he rolled his neck, and her sword sliced along a cheek. Damn! Too close for bladework, the Tiger drove the butt of the axe down onto her collarbone with crushing force. The armor plate saved her shoulder, but shock and pain drove Danica to her knees, her numb hand opening to drop the sword.

"Die," the Tiger hissed, raising the axe high above his head for the final blow.

Chapter Six

Part of Danica's mind, astounded by the opening presented, considered what Mogei would say about such an attack: grave-bait, she could hear the Leopard mutter in disgust. If not for that single, brutal blow to her shoulder, the bounty hunter could have written her name in the Tiger's stomach with the tip of her sword.

The rest of her thoughts were focused on the pain, fighting to move through and past it. With an effort of will she overcame the paralysis of the impact and shooting agony. She released the edge of her cloak, shifting to a fighting grip on the foot-long Chevernaise war knife held in the same hand, concealed until now by the leather. Mail shirt riding up with his raised arms, the mercenary's soft-furred belly was exposed; Danica lunged, driving the heavy blade deep. A burgeoning roar of triumph soared upward into a scream of shock and agony as the axe fell heedlessly from the whiteshield's fingers to the grass beside them. The Tiger's twisted face bent towards her, jaw gaping , finger length canines bared in a last attempt to shred away her life. She cratered him then, twisting the long knife in his wound, not up towards the heart where it would hold him on his feet for that crucial instant, but down with force, driving the point of the blade into the bones in his hips. Falling away off the edged steel onto his backside, mouth open in a keening howl, the Tiger reached for her with hooked claws. Too late. She stepped back and watched as, helpless and harmless, the sellsword sank back, legs splayed out, before rolling over, clutching his abdomen.

Three!

Danica swung around to locate Tucker, hoping to see him standing over the dead body of another mercenary. To her horror, he was leaping away from a sword stroke, desperately dodging and unable to counter with his much shorter weapon. What in blazes? I thought he had the Wolf! She had time for one step in his direction before something, a scent, a whisper of noise, a feeling, ran a cold finger up her spine. For an instant the Fox hesitated, then she knew, and that knowledge sent a silent scream of raw panic tearing through her mind. With a horrified realization of what was surely already shrieking towards her, the bounty hunter threw herself in a spine twisting roll to one side.

It saved her life.

The coruscating sphere of arcane energies whipped past her and bloomed, a deadly flower of searing heat. Fur withering on her legs, Danica felt the skin stretch tautly on one calf. Close to a dozen paces away stood the Wizard, shakily getting to her feet, hand still outstretched after throwing the killing spell. Her hood had fallen back and now her thin, pretty face, fur thickly matted with blood, stared wildly at the Red Fox. Head wound, came the errant thought in Danica's mind as she crouched on the blood-slick grass. Despite the terrific blows she had received, the Weasel remained conscious, regained her footing, and now stared coldly across the space between them. For a heartbeat they stood thus, the bounty hunter poised on her toes, heavy knife held loosely in her left gloved hand and three fingers of her right touching the grass, the Wizard standing thin and straight, short-hafted mace gripped solidly, one eye swollen shut but the other burning with an inner fire. Another beat of the heart, and both women exploded into motion.

Speed, speed, and more speed; Danica pushed herself to the limit, desperately flinging herself across the space at the Wizard to close before the next spell struck home. The wounded Weasel's free hand wove a blurred pattern in the air before her, and a tiny ball of sun-bright flame materialized therein; Danica realized almost too late she could never reach the woman in time. Flexing burned muscle proved painful, but the Fox leapt high, trusting a combat trained spellthrower to aim for the lower body. The point of light hurtled toward her, slicing the air as it warped from a small globe into a thin spike of pure flame. Heat ignited the damp grass below the lance of scintillating fire, forming a doubled blazing thread stretching out from the mage. Danica had no time to appreciate the spell; she was over it and slamming into the Weasel, driving them both to the ground in a tangle of limbs. The bounty hunter worked her blade quickly against the Wizard's body, cutting savagely and looking for an opportunity to drive home a thrust as they struggled, snapping and snarling. The Chevernaise weapon struck light armor and more, repelled from the leather with sparks and a bright chiming. The Weasel kicked Danica off and rolled over, mace fisted and swinging in a high arc, then down again. The bounty hunter pushed off with one hand, sliding out from under the weapon; it struck earth with a flare of light and a blast of heat that singed her whiskers. Well, that tears it. She's no apprentice, and that 'enhancement' to her armor tells me she knows more than fire magic. The hunter whirled to her feet, coming about to face her opponent. Blood dripping from the gashes on her face, the Weasel was up on her knees, already preparing another spell. The triumphant glitter in her eyes told Danica the Wizard was nearly finished.It was the same spell as before, and the sphere of light had just appeared. Thin lips peeled back from the Weasel's needle-sharp teeth, the killing fire lanced out high this time; if the Fox jumped it would all be over. If she went to ground, no doubt the flaming mace would hammer down an instant later.

Danica twisted at the last instant, presenting her left side to the mage and leaning far back on her left foot. At the same time, her left hand snapped up to point at the Weasel's leg. The heavy knife, blade shimmering with reflected light from the spell, flew forward from the underhand throw like a spear. A raging finger of light shot by Danica's chest, just under her throat and above her breasts, the heat flash-igniting her leather armor for an instant, sending brief, searing pain through her body. The Chevernaise war-knife struck the Wizard's thigh point first, driving through the magic protection with the sound of a distant bell and sinking into the woman's unprotected leg. She screamed and staggered, slapping the weapon from her thigh. Her spell, though not fully blocking the knife, prevented a deep wound. Then Danica's gloved hand dug into her collar and dragged her forward. One, two, three elbow smashes into the fineboned features, and the Wizard finally crumpled, deadweight in the bounty-hunter's grip. Danica held her for an instant more, considering, then let her drop as fingers lost their strength. I should kill her. I really should.

Spotting her knife, Danica gathered it up and turned away from the fallen woman. Panting heavily now, pain rippling through her body, she hoped Tucker had managed to get his opponent under control; cuts and wounds were things with which she was woefully familiar and could ignore. Burns were something altogether different.

Her eyes she found the Raccoon, fresh blood streaming from his chest, now frantically rolling away from the hacking sword of the second wolf. Forcing her exhausted body into a sprint, Danica reached the place where she had fought the Tiger. Ignoring his moans she glanced about and found her sword, nearly falling to her knees to grab the hilt. "Hey!" The mercenary, shield forgotten on the ground, spun on her, blade coming to bear. One last cast of the dice, then. Somehow, somewhere, Danica found the strength within to throw off the sodden cloak of exhaustion and pain that had settled over her. Heavy knife in one hand, she began drawing lazy circles in the air with the tip of the light sword in her other.

"Ye bloody reiver! I'll be..." the Wolf began, advancing on her with a wild light in his eyes. Surprisingly, a shout from his brother interrupted him.

"Lad!" the downed Wolf cried, holding a pad of cloth against his shoulder. Bandage from his kit, thought Danica, faintly approving. He must carry it at his belt. "Forget it! Put down yer blasted sword!"

"I canna let her live for what she's done, Camden! Ambushing us, cutting ye down, killing Shaaban!" The boy, for she realized he was definitely the younger of the two, frothed at the mouth, crazed and stinking of rage. For an instant Danica feared he was a barasark, then dismissed the idea. Northerners were renowned for such people, wildmen who set aside self-preservation and rational thought to allow themselves access to the terrible strengths of instinct and rage. Had he been such, he would hardly be carrying a blade and wearing chainmail; more likely he would be sporting a loin cloth or going about naked.

The bounty hunter kept silent; adding her own tongue to the mix would only serve to infuriate the youngster further. If I can finish this without any more blood spilled, that would be good.

Frantic now, the wounded Wolf pounded his injured fist on the ground, spattering blood in wide arcs from the wrist. "She'll gut ye like a trout, Keith! Look around!" Keith stared about wildly, his eyes touching on the battered and unconscious mage and the struggling, moaning Tiger then flicking back to her. Danica shrugged, unconcerned; it cost her a sharp stab of pain and made spots dance before her eyes, but she was sure her weakness did not show.

"Your brother's going to bleed to death without someone to help him." Watching his eyes, she saw him flinch, saw the quick shift from hysterical rage to fear.

"She's going to KILL you, boy! Put up yer cursed sword!" Camden screamed hoarsely, and it finally penetrated. Hand shaking, Keith dropped the blade, and backed away to sink down on the ground beside his brother. Camden began to weep with relief and shock, gripping him tightly. "I thought I'd be taking yer body back to our mother and father, lad," the older Wolf cried. Still trembling with battle rage, Keith angrily thrust his arm away and unbuckled a pouch, glaring at Danica. Ignoring the Wolf, she carefully picked up her sheath and walked over to Tucker on shaky knees. *I can't believe this worked. Heloise, let Tucker still live.* The thief forced a grin as she knelt beside him. "Just a scratch is all," he grunted. But when she pulled his hand away, the blood ran fresh and dark. *Damn. It was a deep puncture into the muscle of his chest, but thankfully did not seem to have hit the lung.* Despite that little bit of luck, a thrust was certainly not a wound to disregard. Without proper care, it would quickly become septic, and Tucker could very well die. Danica needed to get him back to Triskellion as quickly as possible. Additionally, the wound would certainly need immediate cleaning and some sort of stitching; without Desmond handy, she would have to do the job herself.

"What happened? You had him," she said, pulling linen from her own field kit with shaky hands. *This isn't going to be easy, Danica.* Tucker hissed and chittered as she wiped the wound. *Wish I had a razor. The fur should be cleared.*

"I don't know. I couldn't stick him. It just..." His explanation cut off abruptly as his features twisted into a pained snarl, but there really was no more needing to be said. The shame and self-loathing in the young Raccoon's eyes told the story quite well.

Never killed a man before and he froze. It was no surprise when sudden relief swept through her; that, at least, was one bridge she would not have to push him across. "It's not easy, putting steel into a body."

He stared past her. "You seemed to handle that pretty well." Danica followed his gaze to the Tiger, Shaaban, coughing blood and shivering, in shock and dying. Faint horror darkened Tucker's eyes behind his mask. "That's..." Unable to complete the thought, he looked away from the gruesome sight.

"Sit up." She finished wrapping his chest and pushed him back down. "Now don't move, and the bleeding may stop sooner rather than later." *Keep him positive, Danica.* "I have to check the Fox."

The captive had writhed a good ten paces away from where Shaaban had dropped him, displaying a desperate endurance and tenacity Danica found almost admirable. She skirted the Tiger carefully, making sure not to come within reach and keeping her sword in hand. Pausing, the bounty hunter reconsidered her direction. *The Fox is going nowhere. But there's something I have to make sure of NOW.*

Returning to her pack, she snagged a length of leather cord and marched quickly to the Wizard. The two Wolves stiffened, then relaxed when she turned the Weasel over and searched for a heartbeat. It was there and strong, despite the blood soaking her leg. Danica sighed with relief. *Nothing personal here; no reason for either of us to die. Though if things came to that, it would be the other woman, to be sure.*

The only real wounds were the slice in the Weasel's leg and her battered head. The bounty hunter carefully rolled her back and began to bind her hands. *Good mercenaries,* she pondered, studying the wary Wolves. *Smart enough to surrender, loyal enough to consider getting up and having at me again if I was going to murder their employer. How'd they get mixed up with that bleeding filth?* "Your friend's going to die soon," she called to them, "but if you want to try to patch him up, be my guest. Or her, if you don't try anything foolish."

The younger Wolf looked to his brother for guidance. Camden spat once, a disgusted grimace wrinkling his snout. "That bastard? He's been nothin' but trouble since the day the Wizard hired him. Vicious, sick monster. If he were afire, I'd not cross the street to empty my bladder on him." Keith looked shocked, but offered no argument. "But ye have our word we'll nae do aught t' the Lady but stop up her wounds." Danica considered this, then shrugged. Unless one of the them was an adept of Theurgy, and that seemed highly unlikely, the woman would not be stirring for some time.

"Go ahead."

While the young Wolf tended to his employer, Danica hunted through the grass, looking for the purse Tucker had dropped. The stink of leather and metal gave it away. Snatching it up, she pulled out a handful of coin, several denarii and four aureals. She considered the gold thoughtfully. There's a fair reward waiting for me back at Triskellion. With a flick of the wrist she sent two of the aureals spinning through the air to the older Wolf as he tried to make himself comfortable. "Blood debt," the Fox called as Camden picked one up and stared at her suspiciously. "I want nothing between us. Take the coin, find a Church, and offer it to the Light of Truth and Beauty for a healing. But let this end here."

For a moment Danica thought he would pitch it back, but his shoulders relaxed and he tossed them in turn to the watching Keith. "Nothing between us." The sellsword gave a harsh bark of laughter. "Truth be told, I weren't planning on hunting ye down, but this erases much o' the bad feeling. Aeiich...I wish ye'd been nae so hard with the tying of that, lad," he cursed, pressing on the linen wrapping his shoulder.

Keith snorted in disgust as he bent over the Weasel. "Aye, and next time I'll let ye do it alone, then. And ye can tell our mother why ye have only one arm, too." The Wolf walked back to his brother, and Danica replaced him by the Wizard. His bandaging was clean and neat, she noted. I should have had him do Tucker. Checking the woman's bound wrists and gag, she nodded in satisfaction. Tied and injured as the Wizard was, she could do nothing until released.

"Your word on it - you will not follow until at least one day has passed. Even if she awakens."

"Our word." Camden nodded firmly. "I'm in no shape besides, and yon Wizard'll likely have a head like an angry badger come the morrow."

Assuming she doesn't die from bleeding in the skull. Danica put the thought out of her head. Remember the reward. A large sum, to be sure. It's all business. Stilling her doubts, she finally returned to the bound captive, again ignoring Shaaban and his piteous moans for aid. Hopefully it would all be over for him soon anyways, sparing her the effort of giving the Tiger the only help she could.

The Grey Fox had managed another few paces, still hopelessly trying to escape. What on earth? Surely he can't think he's going to get anywhere. And he must know things have changed, that something serious is going on. With her toe, she flipped him over. Tall, lean, dressed in rags of silk and linen; Danica supposed he would be handsome, were it not for the gag filling his mouth, the rolling eyes, and the stink of terror wafting from him in waves. "Calm down. I'm not here to hurt you." At her voice the Grey Fox started and began to writhe violently. Pinning him with a knee, she tugged at the ties of the gag with her gloved hands. It came free and he spat the crumpled cloth onto the grass. "Are you injured? Is there pain?" Worry spiked her voice. It wouldn't do, she rationalized, to have him die before she collected the reward. That's what it's about, Danica. The reward, nothing else.

The Grey Fox stared into the sky with glazed eyes, drew in a deep breath, and began to scream as though the cries were torn from him by iron hooks.

Danica jerked back in surprise, nearly falling as the bound man began to twist and turn again. The howls did not diminish one whit, if anything growing louder. They chilled her blood; screams of agony she could have weathered and had done so before, but these shrieks of pure, raw terror stunned her to the core. The bounty hunter pulled away in horror, stepping back as the bound Fox tore divots in the ground with his claws, sobbing and choking.

Her composure failed utterly and Danica spun on the Wolves, taking in their carefully blank expressions. "What did you bastards do to him?" she screamed, suddenly filled with a mindless fury. They flinched , evidently realizing she teetered on the edge of a killing rage.   "It's nae what ye think!" cried Camden as the bounty hunter stalke towards them pulling steel, leaving the Fox to howl at the sky behind her. "Stop a moment and listen!"

"You'd better talk fast," Danica hissed through gritted teeth, both hands fisted down at her waist, sword tip jutting out at their eye level dancing hypnotically as her hands shook with fury.

"He's been like that since I first laid eyes on him! We bought him from th'slaver, and his mind was fair cheese when Recondrite paid the gold!" The words tumbled out of Keith's mouth as he gestured frantically at the unconscious Wizard. "We've had a cursed difficult time keepin' him along with us; he tries t'run if ye turn yer back on him for a heartbeat!"

"Truth and Beauty, m'lady!" Camden nodded frantically, hands carefully anywhere but near his sword hilt. "He's a bloody lunatic, that one! Screams if ye pin him down, chews through gags all the time, doesn't seem t'ken how to talk - I'm thinkin' I'll be thankin' ye for taking him off our hands!"

The fear on their faces was genuine, equally so the urgency. Danica wished she'd spent more time observing liars; by the time she began a hunt, her quarry's guilt had usually been considered and validated by a court, be it low or high. Truth be told, though, very little of her time went to searching for High Court criminals; few nobles wished to set the precedent of commoners pursuing those of better blood. Wouldn't they be surprised at the truth. Having had little experience dealing with con-artists and the like, Danica could not say for sure that the Wolves were telling the truth, but with what she had observed there was a tiny voice inside counseling

her as to their veracity. After another long, searching look that had them both
panting nervously, she nodded once, curtly. The long, agonized wailing continued
behind her, unabated.

"All right. Say I believe you. What did she, the Wizard, have to say about this?"

"Lady Recondrite?" Camden screwed up his face, evidently trying to remember.
The slowly swaying point of her blade jogged his memory quickly. "Well, from what
she said, and she did cast some kind o'spell on the Fox t'check it; the poor man's got
some kind o'magic on him." His voice dropped and he glanced about nervously.
"She seemed t' think it might be something of a curse."

A curse? Black magic was rare indeed in this time, though if you hearkened to the
Church of S'allumer, all too prevalent in the wicked past. While magic in general
was far from common, Necromancy remained a shadow spoken of in hushed
whispers or fool's tales. Perilous to the souls of both the adept and his enemies, and
outlawed by Church and High Court, Black magic was punishable by death and
worse. One could travel an entire life without seeing evidence of its existence
outside of stories and mothers' threats to their children. And now, in one single
job, Danica had held steel against one Wizard at the bequest of another; she was
gaining a tiny glimpse of some of the darkest of forces one could manipulate.

Unfortunately it had the bounty hunter barely restraining a few choice curses of
her own, of the mundane sort naturally. She wanted to speak to the Grey Fox, not
care for a blithering idiot! Another thought struck her, and Danica turned back to
the wary Wolves. "Did the Lady say if it could jump to someone else?" Both of
them shook their heads. "Did the Lady say it couldn't be?" she clarified, gritting her
teeth.

"She didn't know," returned Keith helpfully. His hopeful smile faded at the look
in her eyes.

"All right," Danica muttered, walking back to the captive. Quickly tying a rope
around his bound wrists for a leash, she leaned close to his head. "Listen to me!"
His cries threatened to drown out her voice. She grabbed his face by the sides and
turned it to look at her. "Listen!" The Grey Fox paused at the sight, mid-howl, and
trailed off into a confused whimper. Probably just surprised at the new face, Danica
thought. "I am here to rescue you," she continued, more quietly with less heat. He
stared at her, tears welling over and pouring into his already damp fur. "Please, be
quiet. We want to help you." It was difficult, speaking to him like this. Danica had
made a habit of being sharp and cold when dealing with her quarry to keep them
fearful of her; never had she needed to handle one softly. No doubt I'm not nearly
as good at it as I was back in childhood. Perhaps nothing she said was sinking into
the Grey Fox; he still wept silently in seeming incomprehension. Slowly she moved
down and slid the knife from its sheath. He watched, shuddering, as she carefully
sliced the cords from his legs. Heloise, please don't let him struggle now. One of
the Wolves shouted a warning; something about the Fox bolting, but she paid it no
heed. The Fox stared down at his ankles as she slowly replaced the blade.
Struggling suddenly, he made it to his feet. Danica surreptitiously put a knee on the
dangling end of the cord binding his wrists, but the filthy man made no attempt at

escape, merely continuing to breathe heavily and stare around through eyes larger than Tucker's. The Wolves' shouts died away to mutterings. "Good," the bounty hunter breathed. "Now, come on. We have to help our friend." She slowly rose to her feet. The Grey skittered away from her to the end of his makeshift leash but did not try to pull away. With a gentle tug he consented to follow her, pulling back only once, when she reached Tucker.

"Tuck, can you walk?"

"If I couldn't, what could we do?" The smile was strained now, but game. "I'm thinking I don't have much choice, Danica. Of course, the hole's in my arm, not my leg, and that makes it a wee bit easier." He extended the other hand, and she took it, letting him pull himself to his feet. The young thief groaned once as wounded muscles shifted, but he managed well enough. Swaying alarmingly for a moment, he caught himself before Danica reached out to help him.

The Grey Fox whined and tried to back away. "Stop that," barked Danica, shortly but not unkindly. "We have to move, now. If a patrol comes by there's nothing to stop them from checking our friends here out, and if they tell the story, we're in big trouble. You can't just go about attacking people on the highway - it's called banditry, no matter what your reason."

"But what if..." Tucker began to counter, staring at the Fox, then fell abruptly silent.

"But what if what?" Becoming tense with worry, Danica felt her temper fraying.

"No, later, it'll keep," he returned, checking around the ground. Kneeling carefully he picked up a thin dagger, and flipped it once, nearly impaling his own palm. Frowning, Tucker carefully slid it into his belt. "Definitely not top shelf," he muttered, the crimson stain across his bandage noticeably larger than before.

"We'll see what we can do about that after we get out of here." Danica took one last look, then stopped. Oh yes. Him. "Stay here. Watch the Wolves."

"Why?" Tucker sounded mildly aggrieved. If this is what the Raccoon became every time he took a blade, she would definitely take better care of him in the future.

"Just do it, Tuck!" Not bothering to wait and see if he listened, she strode swiftly across the damp grass to the bloodstained patch where Shaaban lay. His great body, once so powerful, was now terribly weak and helpless. The massive skull rolled over and his shock-glazed eyes turned to her.

"Help?" he whimpered.

"There's no helping you now," Danica muttered, feeling both disgust and pity. A vicious bastard, but no one deserved to choke out a life like this. Behind her leg, out of his sight, she readied her sword. "Close your eyes."

A tear seeped out as his lids shut.

*   *   *

Chapter Seven

The travois strapped to her shoulders and a wild lunatic with wrists and throat tied to her belt made travel difficult, to be sure. Despite the vicious fight and the accompanying letdown, a few hours of this and the bounty-hunter was ready to kill again. Having no one Danica actively wanted dead within easy reach simply threw another frustration on the growing pile.

Glancing back along the East Road she still saw nothing, for which Heloise earned another brief prayer of thanks. Thus far it was a full day's walk traveled, with several stops to slow them down. One was made to avoid a Rinaldi patrol, two more to avoid the curious eyes of other travelers, and a fourth to eat. After the meal, she had cut up several saplings to make the frame of the travois, which she lashed together with leather thongs. Over Tucker's strenuous objection and protestation that he 'only needed to sit down a bit longer' Danica laid him on the wooden structure, carefully tying him on with more thongs, and began to drag him. The endless jouncing over the cobblestones must have been a nightmare for the thief and he passed out in short order. At least with Tuck unconscious, the bounty-hunter was not subjected to his endless commentary about how he felt well enough to walk. All things considered, it was not a good day for traveling.

She might be halfway to Triskellion, and night was falling.

"That's it." Danica let out a long breath and slowly untied the crude harness, lowering Tucker gently to the ground, "I'm done for the day. Rinaldi patrols, bandits, slavers, even a rogue destrier or two...bring them on." Collapsing to a seated position she watched the Grey Fox skitter away, as far as the leash would allow. You can't stop in the middle of the road, idiot. Get up, dammit. With a groan she forced her weary legs to bear the weight, and carefully dragged the travois from the cobbles. The Grey Fox followed; he had little choice in the matter.

It took her some time to prepare the campsite in the middle of a farmer's field, complete with fire and water, collected earlier from the Tiger's pack, heating atop it. Strips of dried meat went into it with some vegetables; Tucker needed the nourishment and would probably throw up dry food. Danica stole a glance at him. He was awake again, but panting, and there was an unhealthy glaze over his normally bright eyes. He had been unable to eat lunch, first sitting silently and staring at the dry food , then slowly crumpling and sliding off the log. She thought he had been dying. It was clear he had a fever; the wound might be turning foul and this sickness could very well kill him. But that would take a few days at least, and she intended to make Triskellion by nightfall tomorrow at the latest.

"Come here." She pitched her voice a trifle higher than usual, and kept it soft. The Grey Fox crept a little closer. It was easier than chasing him; she discovered earlier that day any unexpected sound or movement produced a disproportionate reaction in him. He shied away from noises in the grass, sudden breezes kept him whimpering in terror, and he absolutely refused to come anywhere near Tucker. Danica thought it might be the scent of blood. She hoped that was it.

She ran a hand over his head and he calmed somewhat, shivering at the touch. Oh yes, definitely magic at work here, some sort of curse laid on the Grey Fox, afflicting him with endless terror. There could be no other reason for such a heightened and constant state of unadulterated fear. She shuddered; such things belonged in children's stories, not burned into this poor lunatic's mind. For the third time that day Danica threaded her gloved fingers through the fur on his cheeks, following their tracks carefully with her eyes and sighing at what she found. No doubt there, much as she wished there would be.

"I'd be jealous, if I didn't feel quite so terrible."

The Grey Fox yelped and jerked her off balance as he darted back to the end of his lines. Danica caught herself to keep from falling and glared at the recumbent Raccoon. "Keep your voice lower. He's easily frightened."

"You've a penchant for stating the obvious, you know?" the burglar grumbled, panting. "And who's the sick one here, anyways?"

She picked up the pot and brought it to him. Beginning to steam, the strips of meat the makeshift stew contained were likely tender now. He turned his nose up, pausing long enough in his gasping to spit. Undaunted, she offered him the thin broth. "You need this, Tuck."

"Not hungry," he muttered, refusing it again.

"Fine," she snapped, slapping the pot down. Hot liquid sloshed over the edge onto one of her gloves and Danica cursed softly, shaking the hand quickly to cool the leather. "Hold still." A quick check of his bandage revealed what she feared. "You're still bleeding."

"You see how well you do, bounced along cursed cobblestones on a couple of poles all bloody day long," Tucker snarled, then flopped back onto the bunched cloak, wheezing. His eyes burned feverishly as he pawed at the wound.

"Stop that." Danica rooted about in her pack, coming out with a string of lizardgut, stretched thin, and a sharp needle wrapped in thick leather. After a moment's thought, she returned to grab a small silver flask of brandy. "Here, start drinking." Tucker eyed it dubiously, sniffed it warily, and then took a cautious sip. The expression on his face was priceless. "Wipe that grin off. I'm not at all pleased at wasting that on you just to keep the pain away." She held the needle in the coals of the campfire for a few heartbeats, then dropped it to the grass, allowing it to cool. Then came the laborious task of threading it with the lizardgut, still wearing her gloves. She noted Tucker enthusiastically polished off the brandy. Not hungry, but always up for drink. He's a man, all right.

"That's Fabrizio de Rinaldi, isn't it?"

Danica almost dropped the needle at Tucker's query. "Why do you say that?" she asked neutrally. There was little sense in denying the truth, unexpected as it was.

"Well, you're being paid a lot of coin," he said, waving his left hand in the air, accent growing more pronounced as the drink and fever took greater hold. "And you haven't yet yelled at him, or got mad, or anything. Sorry to say but that's a wee bit out of character for you. That lot was going to an awful bit o' trouble to take him to the Horses, so they must have known they'd get a chunk of gold. Plus he's

Grey, and rumors say the Don and his sons were killed with magic, Black magic. Lastly, remember we were talking about Fabrizio before we left? So what if he got away, and picked up a wee bit of a curse?"

Always remember, Danica: young and male doesn't necessarily mean stupid. "Well you're right in the center ring with that one." No lie. Just not the whole truth about why she hunted Fabrizio de Rinaldi.

"I knew it." He nodded in satisfaction. "With all of the Guard whispering about it, and then Delaney telling us about Tamurello wanting to find him. Seeing as the moneylender was doing business for the heir, I figure that you're working for Tamurello. He must have realized the 'lackwit' was the real heir. You could have told us, you know." The Raccoon frowned briefly. "You were hired to get him back, weren't you?"

"Yes." Now a lie, and it burned into her throat. In his wounded condition Tucker mixed the facts up completely. He was unable to percieve the holes in his own deduction, making it so much easier for Danica to fool him. Lying to a friend, no less, but the thought of the accusation, the betrayal in Tucker's eyes if he heard the truth was too much to bear. All of the pieces had fallen into place for the bounty hunter herself as soon as she had verified that this actually was Fabrizio de Rinaldi - ridiculously simple, if one knew what to look for. Obviously the false Fabrizio, or more likely his master, had hired her. Hired her to bring back the real Fabrizio, so he could be dealt with. Danica considered her friends: the two Raccoons, an apothecary, and a scholarly cleric. None of them would understand, every one would consider this nothing less than murder. So what would you call it, Danica? Fabrizio was nothing to her, she repeated to herself, nothing. If there were ever any feelings of loyalty in her heart towards the Rinaldi family, they had died during the long years spent on the trail out of Triskellion. But Tucker, Delaney, the others? The thought of losing their friendship stung, more deeply than she expected.

Which was precisely why Tucker's wound needed to be stitched.

"Now, this is going to hurt."

"What are you going t'do?" In his weakened state, the alcohol was hitting the Raccoon like a hammer.

"I'm going to have to cut your wound, Tuck." She finished removing the bandages and stared through his fur at the ugly, oozing pucker. "Punctures don't seal up well when you stitch them. You have to slice them first."

"You're going to...cut it?" Tucker's face fell sharply. "Well, it couldn't be any worse than how I feel now," he managed in a ghastly attempt at bravery.

One of Tucker's sharper daggers went into the fire next. "It won't take but a second, Tuck." Her stomach already churned at the idea of putting steel to her friend. She brought the weapon out of the fire and stared at its smoking blade. Heloise, can I do this? A few heartbeats while the blade cooled were all she had time for. Staring into the Raccoon's resolute, but terrified eyes she hoped the fever and the drink would take the edge from the pain.

They did, somewhat.

The initial cut went well, with the burglar's only reaction a savage hiss through gritted teeth. Blood flowed thick and dark, and Danica pressed the linen against the wound hard to wipe it away. With the new cut, the puncture's shape changed from a hole to a bulging gash. Now she could safely stitch it.

Tucker, despite further attempts at stoicism, finally succumbed and passed out, though not until the job was almost complete. Danica cheerfully cursed him; he should have gone ahead and given up at the very beginning rather than toughing it out that far. It would have been easier on him, and her as well. Quickly she stripped off the gloves and took up the needle. Now, freed of their constraints, her hands' stitching was fast and sure. After some time, while tying off the final knot, some sense, perhaps hearing or smell, gave a faint warning. The stitches being her first priority, Danica finished them before slowly turning her head.

Fabrizio, wrists worn near furless but also distinctly ropeless, crouched behind her, ears flattened in sudden fear, and feet ready to flee. *How long has he been free? I should have checked his damned bonds!* Another, more intriguing thought occurred to her. *And how long has he been sitting there?* His eyes, she saw, slowly slid down her arms to rest on her hands. Danica failed to suppress a flinch but stubbornly refused to snatch up the gloves. She glared defiantly until the madman lowered his head, turning away his shame-filled gaze. *Well, there is a brain inside that skull after all,* she mused, cocking an eyebrow in surprise. *I never expected to get that kind of a reaction out of him.*

"What in the name of the Light happened to your hands?"

Tucker's horrified exclamation froze both her and Fabrizio; fortunately, the Grey Fox did not run. The only thing keeping her from the gloves now was the crushing knowledge it was far, far too late. Danica slowly looked down, at the hands she saw only when bathing.

The wrists were slim, despite constant work with the heavy Chevernaise fighting knife and her dead mentor's blade. They tapered delicately down into hands with fur pale and fine, never having been exposed to the sun, and worn away under the thin but ever-present leather. Artist's fingers stretched out from her palms, slender and light, dexterous and cunning...ending in poorly healed, gaping scars where claws had once grown.

Clawless.

Danica stared at the offending digits, despondent, a sudden wave of disgust and self-hatred sliding through her veins like greased offal. Any pledge to keep silent about her secret that she could extract from Tucker would hold for exactly the amount of time it took to reach Triskellion. He would promptly blurt out her shame to Porter, Desmond, or worse, any drunken patron of the Crested Mastiff, with no regard for former promises or impending consequences. Fantastic at keeping his own secrets, the burglar was the world's worst confidant. Oddly, there was a faint thread of relief coursing through her at that moment. Despite whatever might come in the future, there would be no need to hide the ugly truth from her friends any longer.

Hard on the heels of that realization came the crushing thought that after this little job, she might have an even more loathsome secret to conceal.

Danica forced herself to meet his gaze. There it was, the pity. Stop it, damn you! "It was a long time ago," she said aloud, holding her voice steady. It took far more effort than she expected; this was the first time in her life the hunter ever spoke about her scars. "I did something my Father didn't particularly appreciate. He had this done in return." And after crippling me, he threw me out on my ears. "You asked me why I don't sing? I stopped then. End of story." No more lullabies for my brother, or for me.

Tucker opened his mouth, his jaw working. Either the burglar was simply unable to think of something to say he considered adequate in his drunken, suffering state, or the look in her eyes put him off. Perhaps it was a bit of each. Regardless, the Raccoon closed his mouth with a snap, nodded once, and turned over. Danica swung away to find Fabrizio staring at her mournfully. He reached out a trembling finger to one of her hands, snatching it back as she jerked her own away violently.

"Quit it," she hissed in annoyance, yanking on her gloves. "Why do you look so cursed sad? They aren't your hands, and it wasn't your doing that this happened to me." The Grey Fox drew back nervously but showed no sign of running away. Good thing too. This little job's already cost me a great deal. Maybe more than it's worth. She stared at Tucker's shoulders. From his breathing, the thief was still awake, but his back remained resolutely towards her, scent undecipherable through the cloying stench of blood. Clawless. She could not even blame him. Claws and self-respect; even most criminals still had theirs.

Just like Mo-gei said - finish the job, she thought wearily, poking the fire. Think of the gold. She sniffed the night air. And Malik. He's out there somewhere, waiting.

The Grey edged a little closer to her. Fabrizio. Say it Danica, his name is Fabrizio. Hard to get the mind around it, as if not knowing his name somehow made her plans more palatable. Deep in her gut, she knew exactly who the Fox was, exactly who she was delivering to his enemies. I could run. I could take him and run, I suppose. "A job taken is a job finished." Words of her mentor, words she lived by all of her life as a hunter. If she backed out now, took him away, who would ever hire her again? The news would spread; there was no way around that. If not the truth, then rumor. And without her trade, how would she pay for them both to live? How could she continue her trade with a crazed, cursed lunatic tagging along, no matter who he was?

It was impossible, not even worth consideration. Besides, with his mind gone this way, death would probably be a blessing in the end.

No matter how hard she tried to convince herself, she could not make that one stick. A faint thread of music, a lullaby, spun in her imagination.

The job. Keep your mind on the gold and the job.

Chapter Eight

The morning failed to become any easier on the travelers.

Danica kept watch the night through. It was not impossible that the wizard, cheated of her prize, would seek them out in the darkness and attempt to reclaim Fabrizio. Not impossible but also not likely, however. With that many cracks on the head the Weasel no doubt nursed a monstrously sick stomach along with a concussion. Without her mercenaries, the woman would be hard pressed to catch up to the bounty hunter, much less force her to give over the Rinaldi noble. Still, a knife across the throat as one slept could be accomplished by a child, or a woman half dead on her feet, and there was no guarantee the wizard was unskilled in Theurgy. A quick healing, and the Weasel would suddenly become a credible threat.

Worse still was the ever-present danger of Malik. Danica suspected he would wait until he could look her in the eye, let her know exactly what was happening, but one could never tell with the unpredictable Coyote. Better to remain awake and aware the night through, despite her exhaustion.

Not to mention that remaining awake kept her out of reach of the dreams she knew waited in sleep.

Thus it was, worn out and ill-tempered, Danica shouldered the travois early the next morning after a hasty meal shared with her two charges. Fabrizio had begun to respond to his name; he came when called and showed no sign of wishing to escape, practically following on Danica's heels. The irony nearly sickened her. She decided to let him remain unbound; not having him linked to her belt was far easier for all three travelers.

Though Tucker's bleeding had stopped, his fever continued to climb and the wound had become puffy, the skin an angry red. Tainted. He even began to rave a bit, babbling about his friends and his sister. Hopefully he would forget the night before completely. She needed to return him to the city at once, where, with proper donations to the Church the Raccoon could receive the necessary help through the miracles of Theurgy. Better yet, let Porter be back from one of his little expeditions. At least then the healing would be without cost. Self-disgust warred with practicality over that last thought and lost.

She carefully put out of her mind the other consequences of returning to the city.

"You're a real hero, Dani." Tucker blathered as they marched (well, as she marched), repeating to himself over and over, like a man with a bellyful of ale, "Going out like this to bring back our lord. I mean, even though you're doing it for gold, you're doing it, right?"

"Right Tuck." She resolutely ignored the twinges his youthful idealism produced, just as she ignored his bastardization of her name. Just this once. "I'm doing it." I'm bringing him back to the slaughter. She glanced at the cursed Fox, finding his eyes, as always, carefully watching her as they traveled. It was as if the madman considered her some kind of savior, and she detested it.

"C'mon, sing a song, Dani. It'll pass the time." When she shook her head in annoyance the Raccoon began himself, belting out a pub tune; his grasp of the melody was execrable. The poles on her shoulders vibrated alarmingly. Fabrizio scampered a few paces away, dancing around nervously. Unable herself to flee, she rolled her ears back in a vain attempt to mute the sound. The Grey Fox whined at her piteously. Danica shook her head; it was better to let Tucker sing, to keep his mind off the pain. There was no more brandy.

The singing broke off abruptly, almost ominously. Dancia considered putting the travois down to check on Tucker when he spoke up. "It looks like...he likes you," he mumbled, voice hoarse. "Hasn't tried to run away from you; even slept by your feet last night."

"He did?" Damn. I never noticed he got that close. I can't be getting used to him already! The guilt was back, stronger than ever. Curse it! He has no reason to feel that way - he should hate me, damn him. Look what I'm going to do to him!

"Sing a song, Dani." The nickname made her grind her teeth and glance at Fabrizio, but there was little in those roving eyes but fear. "He wants you to sing a song, too." The cursed noble actually seemed to understand, looking up at her for a moment, then snapping his head away and yipping incoherently as a snake slithered across the cobbles ahead. For an instant an image burst into her mind, the same as that of the night before. Singing lullabies to her brother. Long ago, before her father threw her out. She quashed it, ruthlessly. Now is not the time to start developing a conscience.

"Sorry Tucker." Danica motioned ahead. "We're in sight of the walls. Almost home." Indeed, she could make out the beginnings of the morning traffic out of Triskellion ahead, the dark shadow of the city proper looming through the morning haze. The farmers' crops and patures began to give away to cleared, rocky fields. Their exhausting travel nearly done, still there was no sign of Malik. What is he thinking? What's his game?

After careful consideration she called Fabrizio over and fit her spare traveling cloak around his neck, pulling up the hood. It wouldn't do, Danica thought, to have him recognized in a chance meeting with a familiar guard. Though it was unlikely any would actually give him a second glance in his ragged clothing, ill luck could always play a role. She caught herself humming quietly as gloved fingers tied the cloak about his throat. The nobleman suffered her attentions with faint frustration, rolling his eyes to keep watch as best as possible over the surrounding terrain. With the cloak there would be no problem now. Worst case, the gate guards would look at Tucker and herself, rather than Fabrizio.

Silencing her humming, Danica began the final leg of the journey, every stride bringing Triskellion's walls into clearer focus. She never thought her relief could be so great at the sight of the accursed place.

Only Fabrizio spoiled her sense of satisfaction, skittering along beside her and gawking at the massive stone fortifications ahead.

*   *   *

81

The city streets rang with festivities. Cheerful as they were, the gate guards were easy to ward off with a quick story about a hunting accident and a trip to the healers. Once inside the walls, song surrounded the travelers, along with many drunken, enthusiastic merrymakers. Danica found herself snarling at some to stop them from 'helping' her drag Tucker to the Crested Mastiff, or from pushing the travois from her shoulders and carrying her off to dance. Vendors offered free food, the meals cheap but still filling, and mugs of watered-down ale or mead; for a wonder, many upstanding citizens took time from their work to accept the largess and stopped to gossip. Here and there Danica spotted the troubled face of a member of one of the other Great Houses; a Doloreaux merchant, or a traveling Avoirdupois Chevalier. No doubt the news of good fortune for Triskellion failed to bode well for their royalty. As well it might.

It seemed that Fabrizio de Rinaldi, son of the late Don, had appeared and declared himself.

The Fabrizio with them, of course, showed no sign of comprehension of the events surrounding him. His entire concern at the moment seemed to be sticking as close to Danica as possible, nearly tripping her every time he shied away from a hollering merrymaker or group of dancers. Tucker, however, lapsed into an ominous silence as they moved through the city streets, his feverish mind no doubt wrestling with the news, attempting to make sense of it. Danica contented herself with keeping them moving towards their goal: Old Town, and the safety of the Inn. The one thing uppermost in her over-full, very troubled mind was Malik. If he were near, the other hunter would have to move soon. Once they entered the Crested Mastiff, the Coyote would be a fool to attempt stealing her prize. With Tucker safe and Delaney backing her up, Danica was confident she would come out on top in any confrontation with her ex-partner. She tried very, very hard to avoid considering what burglar must be thinking. She almost succeeded.

Once through the gates of Old Townand nearing her goal, Danica began to feel her tension rise. The walls of the Rinaldi Keep dominated the edge of the sky before them; to their right, the old watchtower jutted up in the distance like a broken tooth. Heart pounding, she increased the pace, pulling harder on Fabrizio's arm and feeling the straps of the travois bite into her shoulders with every step. A few hoots and cries of derision drifted to her from the bystanders on the streets; the festivities were much less rowdy here, with more people simply taking advantage of the occasion to drink themselves insensible. Not that many of the citizens out needed that particular excuse at the best of times. The Rinaldi and their jockeying for power mattered much less here in Old Town; things would be just as poor under any other ruler.

Danica cared nothing for those hurling insults; they were no danger. Hissing lizards usually fled when confronted; it was the silent, deadly cobras that were the real threat. If she kept to the open streets....

Another crowd of revelers swept up on her from behind, surrounding her with splashing tankards of foul smelling ale, deafening howls, and cries of drunken exuberance. Tightening her grip on Fabrizio's arm, Danica opened her mouth to curse them off...then stopped. A light, ticklish feeling by her hip, the tingle of something touching skin in between her chest armor and greaves, turned her insides to water. A cold tickle. A steely tickle, easily capable of threading up to her kidney in one crimson instant.

"My thanks, Danica," breathed the voice in her ear, breath redolent of foreign spices. "Do not release my package; you brought it all of this way for me, now you may bring it one or two steps closer. It may even make you feel better about losing." The revelers passed, leaving them alone in the middle of the street save for a few curious onlookers. She could count on no help from them; the only reason they might call the Guard would be to increase the entertainment value.

"Funny," she rasped back, voice quivering slightly. "I thought I would smell you coming."

"Saaaaa, Danica, how rude of you." Malik stepped around to her side, out of reach of Tucker. As if the near crippled Raccoon posed any danger. "You know I am careful to wash before every job and not use any of my usual perfumes."

"I smelled you by my campsite."

"As you were so meant to do," he returned, absently, staring across her at the Grey Fox tugging frantically at her gripping hand. "I wanted you to push forward, hard. Do my work for me. And you obliged me so very well. Certainly you did not disappoint against the Wizard." For an instant Danica was tempted to release Fabrizio, but Malik would put the blade into her kidney and be on top of the madman in a flash. "Off the main pathway." The Coyote jerked her arm, and she dragged Tucker and Fabrizio towards one of the smaller alleys leading off the main course of Old Town, where the aqueduct burbled merrily.

"Danica," came Tucker's groan. "What's happening?"

The bounty hunter had to lick her lips and swallow once to answer him. "Malik. The one I told you about." She silently cursed her cracking voice; beside her Fabrizio picked up on the fear and clung to her arm, eyes wide in terror. Tucker pulled in a pained breath.

"What...I'll...," he muttered, beginning to thrash about on the travois.

"Tucker, stop!" she ordered, heedless of Malik's appraising glance. "You'll hurt yourself!" He quieted, thankfully, and she looked her erstwhile partner in his smiling face, meeting his empty eyes as they stepped along the track, under the shadows of the buildings to either side. "You leave him out of this, you hear? He's nothing to do with it, and doesn't even know you."

"He does now," whispered the Coyote thoughtfully. She tensed, and the needle point of the stiletto, still precisely where it was first laid, jabbed slightly. Danica felt a single drop of blood well up. "So, that is how it stands between the two of you, eh? My people have punishments for unmarried women who do such things."

For a moment a wave of fury obliterated her fear; the Red Fox would be damned before she bothered to explain things to the murderer. "I bet it isn't as bad as getting thrown out of the tribe, Malik," she snarled in return, feeling a surge of petty satisfaction at seeing his eyes widen in surprise and rage. "What did you do there, murder more children?"

"Ah, back to that, as always," he muttered, but she could feel the metal against her side tremble with his anger, and her own guttered, blown out by a sudden gust of mortality. Oh fantastic, Danica. Infuriate him. Make absolutely sure he's going to kill Tuck. "Stop here."

She did, and with his left hand he unbuckled her belt, letting it fall to the ground. Fingers slid impersonally around her back, and pulled the Chevernaise blade from its hanging sheath; two quick slashes cut the travois away, first spilling Tucker off, then dropping the poles to the ground. The Raccoon groaned when he hit the cobblestones, and Fabrizio fought silently to free himself from her grasp before huddling against her leg, shuddering. Oh, Heloise, it's going to be both of them. Tucker, leaping down this deadly well without any clue how deep it went, just to help her. And Fabrizio. Despite her decision to fulfill her contract, the thought of handing him over to Malik turned her stomach. For an instant Danica considered throwing herself against the Coyote; self-preservation remained a powerful instinct, though, as it had been for many years now. When the thin blade pricked her again, she froze, unable to force herself to move. A flick of a Malik's wrist sent the heavy Chevernaise knife spinning across the alley. Danica winced as the blade hit the cobbles, but then realized a damaged weapon would probably not matter in a few heartbeats.

"Now, push Fabrizio de Rinaldi against the wall, please." Danica did so, and the small blade moved around her back with Malik. A quick shuffle, a thud, and Tucker let out a high pitched, eerie groan; with mounting resignation she realized the Coyote had kicked the Raccoon in his wound to keep him occupied. Nothing she could do here; any resistance would kill her that much sooner. It was surprising Malik had waited this long to thrust the dagger home. A leather thong was pushed into her hand. "Rope him."

Danica slowly reached out and gripped the Grey Fox's wrists. Carefully the Red Fox tied them together, fully aware of Malik's watchful eye. "His feet too." A longer thong fell across her shoulder, and she hobbled the fox. Malik shoved her suddenly, forcing her face down, and struck, driving the hilt of the dagger into the back of Fabrizio's neck. The fear-crazed noble dropped, stunned, as Danica rose to her knees.

"Are you planning on fighting me fairly?" She hated the trembling in her voice. Normally the Red Fox could face naked steel without flinching, but the same steel in Malik's hands took on sinister undertones, as if his corrupt spirit infected the metal. If he let her pick up her own blade, however,....

A short bark of laughter shattered that hope. "Are you mad? This is not a game, Danica." He sneered. "We are not here to discover which of us is more capable with a sword. That question has been answered time and time again," he finished, shaking his head sadly. It was true enough. With that many more years of experience under his belt, and a natural gift for sudden violence that the Fox simply could not match, Malik outclassed her. But there would have been a chance. As if reading her mind, he continued. "Anyone can be lucky once, Danica. From our past association I know I can beat you four out of five passes with wooden blades. But these are live steel, and my confidence in myself is sufficient that I will not risk that fifth pass to prove myself your better one last time." Abruptly his ears perked, and he paused, attention diverted slightly. But not enough, curse it!

"Is this private?" drawled a voice from deeper in the alley. Both bounty hunters glanced that way to see a group of hunched silhouettes filling the cramped passage, led by a hard-eyed Badger wearing scraps of ill-fitting armor. One of the innumerable alley-gangs thriving in the streets of Old Town, they fed off its citizens like leeches, dodging the Guard, and occasionally starting a small war with another such group. The leader took a step forward, holding out one hand. "You're on our territory, m'friend, but you're also in luck. We don't want any trouble, y'hear? After all, it's a festive time!" The Badger leered and licked his lips. "I figure if you're going to bleed her, might as well hand her over to us instead - we can take care of that...after. Add your silver, and we let you go with everything else you've got, even your life." Grinning, he showed off a set of broken and decaying teeth. "Not a bad bargain, eh? What do you say?" From behind the Badger's wide shoulders came rumbles of agreement, and the faint glimmer of drawn steel. Danica's blood turned to ice.

The scimitar slid silently from its scabbard, with never a sound. It swung up to point squarely at the gang leader's face; the knife pressed through Danica's fur against her skin never twitched. "You made one mistake," Malik said quietly. "You took the front. So you die first."

Danica could see the Badger prepare to utter a, no doubt, angry rebuttal. Then the words struck home and he stopped, mouth opening and closing spasmodically. Having looked very deeply into Malik's eyes herself, the Red Fox knew exactly what he was seeing...death. To Malik, the Badger was simply one more obstacle to be removed; there was no concern there, only faint annoyance at the disturbance. The gang leader took a step back only to realize that his retreat was blocked by his own men. For them to attack, he would be forced to scrabble, ignominiously, through their ranks while ordering them to fight. Such a display would be the death knell for his position. Trapped before what amounted to a force of nature, the brute's resolve melted like snow under summer sun. Quietly the gang leader held up both hands, slowly pushing backwards. "C'mon lads. It's not worth bleeding over. Let's leave the man to his work." A few dissatisfied murmurs rose behind him. "Move!" he shouted, squelching the opposition.

In a few heartbeats the alley returned to its former silence.

"Filth," muttered Malik as Danica felt her shoulders slump with an odd relief. "There. The reason I entered this sort of work." The Red Fox could only stare up at him, stunned by his words. Spoken absently, they held the ring of truth. Then Malik...he started doing this for the same reasons as me. At one time he believed he did good. When had that changed for him? For that matter, when had it changed for her? How long since I cared about why I was hunting, beyond the fact that there was money offered?

"Turn around," whispered the Coyote. With no choice, Danica did as he bid. "Kneel."

This was death. "Malik," she began, her voice hoarse with fear.

He kicked her behind the knee, all the while keeping the cold steel against her side. The Fox dropped to the ground, and the blade withdrew. Still she found herself unable to move.

"Malik, please. Think about this. You've won." The words spilled from Danica's lips before she could clamp them shut. Begging Malik. He must be laughing inside. Lying in front of her, Fabrizio craned his head, trying to see what was going on.

"You took from me my friend, Danica. The only one on this accursed island I cared for. The only one who accepted me for who I was, you took from me." The Coyote's words dripped with vitriol; she could taste the hatred. She could scent his exaltation.

Suddenly tired of being afraid, Danica felt a fresh wave of loathing for this monster crest and wash away the fear. "Mo-gei never knew you; he didn't know what you were until I showed him. A sadistic killer. That's when he turned away from you, you vicious monster." It would get her killed, but she felt a certain satisfaction in her refusal to cower any longer. It seemed Malik always managed to goad her into anger, whatever the situation.

"Oh, yes, you showed him. You knew full well what I had planned, but you didn't have the courage to face and stop me, did you Danica?" The oily sense of victory was back in his voice as his words cut; she shivered with the memory. "Yes, you knew what I was about, did you not? You knew what I was, what I would do with the children, but you did not try to stop me. Instead, you ran to Mo-gei, after the fact, to show him what I had done. So you could show him what a 'vicious monster' I was and not have to travel with me any more."

"I couldn't have stopped you," Danica gasped, anger draining away under the relentless hammering of his words on her conscience. What little I have left. "I was young. You were so much better than me. I would have died."

"No," Malik crooned almost tenderly, "the important fact is you would have tried. In the face of such a horrible crime, as you call it, any 'good' person would, yes? But you did not, did you? You waited. I freely admit I killed them, but I took a contract to find them, lawbreakers that they were. For you they were more, and your conscience told you it was wrong. Yet you did nothing. So tell me, Danica, kneeling there so sure of your righteousness, who is also to blame for the deaths of those children?"

The Fox's only answer was harsh breathing as her mind desperately tried to think of something, anything, to refute the Coyote's conclusion. Nothing came.

"And now? Fabrizio de Rinaldi? Knowing your background, I am rather shocked, Danica." The amusement in his tone fell against numb ears. She was almost beyond caring now. "And this one, this stripe-tailed bandit? A friend, perhaps? Or do you even have friends, Danica?" His breath grew warm on her ear, the Coyote's mouth close as he whispered. "I would have DIED for Mo-gei. And you refuse to even fight for these two. Scheming, no doubt, for one last chance to save your own hide. You are still but a child, caring only for your own life, only for your own needs. Always assuming things will turn out for the best. Your best." A shift in his body moved him back, and Danica could imagine him readying his blade. "No matter; dream your pleasant dreams of escape. They will be brief, and the long-awaited justice, the retribution, for my loss will be mine. The gold," he gloated, "is merely a bonus." He moved to the side slightly; she could see him now, staring down at her, the scimitar a bright wing of steel between them. It rose...and then she saw her sword.

Mo-gei's blade lay on the cobblestones in its sheath, still attached to her belt, less than a pace from Malik. In it rested her chance, the only chance to save herself, all of them, from the remorseless Coyote. His scimitar rose higher, reaching its apex, when suddenly she leaped, snatched the belt, and rolled along the ground with it swinging in her hand. Danica heard no clang of metal on the cobbles behind her; Malik must have checked his swing. She spun to her knees, hand grabbing for her sword hilt...and coming up with only air.

The scabbard was empty.

Horrified, she turned back to find Malik still frozen in the same stance, only his head turned towards her. His right foot, however, stood on the sword's hilt. He stepped on it, and I pulled the scabbard right off the blade!

"Surprised? You should not be. Faster than I you may be, Danica, but as always I am one step ahead in mind and body. Well, almost always." His smile faded for a moment. "There was that one time with the children, yes?" With two swift steps he crossed the distance and flicked the belt from her unresisting hands. "You are so terribly easy to predict, Danica. Do you know why?" The curved edge kissed her neck; she shook her head slowly, carefully. "Because you are the same as I in many ways, yes?"

"No," Danica whispered.

"I think," he countered, "we both know the truth. Goodbye, Danica." He tensed, and she could sense what he planned. He would simply open her throat with the edge of the blade. There would be no long windup and much less mess. The Fox tried to move, but with steel against throat her body was paralyzed, refusing to take any chance, desperate for one, last breath.. She could only wait for the pain and pray it would be quick.

A sudden grunt, an ugly, slippery noise, and crimson rain pattered down on the wet cobbles. Danica's eyes opened wide, wider than the enormous slash through Malik's throat. The scimitar fell away from her neck, and the Coyote tumbled against the wall, shoved violently from behind. Tucker staggered back, leaning against the opposite side of the alley, face drawn, whiskers quivering with effort. The bandage wrapping his shoulder seeped red. "Bastard...talks too much," the Raccoon gasped at her, then stared at his hands in horror. They were slick with the Coyote's blood. Malik sagged slightly, life running away in long rivulets of red, and tried to raise his curved blade. It slipped from weakening fingers and clattered to

the cobbles.

Danica stood shakily, muscles weak, and caught Tucker as he began to fall.
"Tuck!"

"Is it true, Danica?" His eyes searched hers, but she could not for her life read
them. They closed in the sleep of unconsciousness before she could discern the
intent of his question. There were, after all, far too many possibilities.

Whimpering, Fabrizio crawled to her side, hands still tied together. With a curse,
she snagged her knife and slashed him free; a few heartbeats later they stumbled
down the alley towards the main road, Tucker slung over her shoulder like a sack of
grain. The sky chose that moment to open up on them, full force; the deluge
obliterated visibility and added stones to Tucker's weight. Danica kept a firm grip
on Fabrizio. It made for slow walking, but it was safer in this downpour. Though
her skin crawled, her back wide open to a blade, she never looked back.

Behind them the rain began to slowly wash the trail of blood from Malik's
sprawled body.

*   *   *

The Inn was packed with the common people, thieves, prostitutes and sundry
other denizens of Old Town pushing their way in and out to celebrate the city's
good fortune. Any excuse for a party would be taken, for there was normally little to
celebrate in Old Town. Despite the rain coming down in driving sheets, a great
many of the patrons sat outside under the cracked and dripping wooden awning,
soaked but uncaring in their cups.

Seeing no hope of shoving her way in while carrying Tucker and leading Fabrizio,
Danica took the alley around the back to the door into the kitchen. Quickly rolling
the burglar to the ground, she hammered on the locked portal with the hilt of her
knife. "Delaney!" the Fox howled over the muted roar of the rain, with diminishing
hope of being heard. Fabrizio whined and shied away from her pounding hand, but
kept one of his looped through her belt. He waited there as Danica beat on the
door and screamed, not even moving when she graduated to kicking the offending
barrier.

When the door finally opened, the bounty hunter had to stumble around on one
foot for a moment to avoid kicking Armande in the shins. "Begone, you filthy-" the
tall horse began in a strong Avoirdupois accent, before his mouth dropped open
and he goggled openly. "Tucker?"

"Pick him up!" ordered Danica through a throat made raw by too much yelling.
Armande stared down at the wounded Raccoon nervously.

"Delaney has left to purchase more brandy, and I am all alone on the bar," he
started, before Danica caught his arm and spun him against the wall. The tip of the
Chevernaise knife hung in front of his eye. The Horse stared, almost too fascinated
by the slick metal to be frightened.

"Listen, part-timer. Pick him up. Carry him in to his room. Then go and wait for
Delaney. You don't," she hissed, "and I'll be juggling your eyeballs in a heartbeat."

The bartender swallowed, eyes crossing again at the razor sharp point as it was withdrawn from his face. Bending quickly, he hefted Tucker and hastened back inside. Danica carefully pried Fabrizio's rigid hand from her belt and followed.

Armande carried Tucker down the back hall to his room on the first floor, beside his sister's and across the hall from Delaney's. Though the innmaster was out, Seanna might be able to give them a hand. Danica would endure any number of barbs concerning her choice of lifestyle if it meant a bit of aid with the wounded Raccoon. Nodding at her door, Danica received a shake of the head from the Horse as a reply. "Out making the world safe for the common folk," she muttered, ignoring Armande's brief flash of anger. *Idiot probably thinks she walks on water, like everyone else does.*

Laid carefully on the bed by the Horse, Tucker's limp body presented a pathetic sight. *He looks so small! Heloise, I hope Desmond or Porter are here, or in town.* "You can go tend bar now," she said absently to the Horse, who left in an almost palpable cloud of relief. There was a rag on the dresser beside a water pitcher. When she motioned, Fabrizio actually went and brought them to her, as eager to please as any trained lizard. Soaking the cloth in water, the Fox laid it on Tucker's head before leaning back and stretching. Her body ached, cold to the bone. Wet, bruised, cut, and burned, it was near giving out, she knew. Carefully the bounty hunter picked up a towel from a pile on the floor of the room, shaking her head sadly. *Why do men never think even to throw them over a chair?* Tossing the towel over Fabrizio's head, she dried his sodden fur; eyes covered, he shivered in fear but permitted the attention. Danica carefully gripped his head in her hands and scrutinized him; the grey and white fur stood up in spikes, and she couldn't hold back a chuckle. It died as she finally paused to consider the brief and lethal violence in the alley.

Malik was dead. Another link with her past snapped. A deep stillness settled over the Red Fox, akin to sadness. Though Danica had not exactly lived in fear of the Coyote, the knowledge that Malik was out there somewhere, thinking of her as he studied the stars and sharpened his blades, always brought a certain...tension to her life. Now that the tension had disappeared, Danica's memory of the Coyote's face was growing dim. Despite their history, the abrupt change in her life brought with it a sense of loss. The loss, however, was mixed with relief, a feeling she suspected would grow ever stronger as time went by.

Who could have known he had me figured so well? The bounty hunter sighed deeply. Every word the Coyote had spoken struck like a ball from a gun. *But is what he described actually me, or just what Malik thought of me?*

"Danica?" The Fox froze, catching her breath. "I guess I've done it now, eh?" The voice came cracked and broken; even Fabrizio seemed affected, turning his head to look at Tucker sadly. Danica raised her eyes to the Raccoon, lying on the bed and staring at the ceiling. He slowly held up his hand and opened the fingers wide. Thick blood clotted there, where the rain failed to reach. "I guess I've used them now." For a moment she was confused, then recalled their conversation around the fire and nodded.

90

His knives.

"Yes, Tuck, I guess you have." Emotions warred within her, the relief and faint sadness over Malik's death and new fear mixed with pity for the young Raccoon. Killing was easy; it was the thinking afterward that was the hard part. It should be the other way around. Fabrizio glanced at her, then gently reached out and took Tucker's fingers, staring at the blood soaking them. He shuddered once, looking back at Danica mournfully, before carefully removing the cloth from the burglar's forehead and painstakingly wiping the blood off the hand and claws. Danica sucked in her breath and stood up, arms wrapped tightly around her stomach.

There IS something there; he has a mind, buried beneath the curse and all of that fear. A storm of indecision, harder even than the rain outdoors, struck her. How could she turn him over, knowing that fragments of the true Fabrizio had survived the curse? And if he were not Fabrizio di Rinaldi...would she feel the same about turning him over to his murderer's claws?

"I have a bit of a question for you." She turned to face Tucker's feverish eyes, bright behind the black mask. His nose twitched uncontrollably. When she nodded carefully, terrified at the thought of what he might ask after all he had heard during their short travels together, he continued. "Why were your claws...taken?"

Danica stood slowly to buy some time, relief fighting with a sick hollowness in the pit of her stomach. Not a question she wanted to answer, it was nevertheless not the question she was dreading. Perhaps if she gave in to this one, the hunter reasoned, he might not ask the other. Perhaps if she told him, he might keep his mouth shut about her claws. And perhaps he had earned an answer, bought with pain.

Sitting on the edge of the bed, she tried not to look at Fabrizio, who was carefully worrying at the blood trapped under Tucker's claws and trembling wildly at the crescendos of singing and shouting emanating from the taproom. Between being tied up and carried for days, the violence back on the road, and Malik's vicious attack, Danica supposed the curse on him was working at a fevered pitch. It's probably tearing at his mind like a pack of northern bethrach lizards. Despite her best efforts, guilt began to burn deeply into her spirit.

"It's a bit of a long story, Tuck," she hedged. It would not do to appear eager to tell it. Well, perhaps eager wasn't the right choice of word. Danica didn't want him to see how relieved she was to be explaining her scars. Better the one story than the other. Better to tell him how she lost her claws, tell him of her older crimes and losses, than to tell him of the true purpose for catching the Fox, the true purpose for bringing Fabrizio de Rinaldi back to Triskellion. Shame in the past could be forgiven; selling a life could not.

"I seem to have time," he returned dryly. She smiled weakly at his feeble attempt at humor. Danica studied his eyes, noting their clear, unblinking gaze, and a shadow of apprehension lessened her relief. Despite the fever, he doesn't seem that confused. Closing her own eyes she drew in a breath, let it out slowly to calm both her heartbeat and her concerns, and began.

Chapter Nine

Staring down at Tucker in the bed before her, his bright, clever eyes locked on hers, Danica traveled back to her youth to find words for her story. Not a terribly difficult task as ever since she had re-entered Triskellion and accepted this commission, the dreams returned, deviling her every night. It would almost be a relief to finally release part of the story into another's keeping, even if Tucker would only keep it long enough to gift it to the next person he met. With luck, the telling of her past might weaken the hold the nightmares had on her sleep.

"When I was young, I had quite a temper. I think it came from being the bastard child of a servant in a noble house. I was tormented endlessly for not having a legitimate father, and I always knew that except for an accident of birth I could have been living pretty well. It got me into a lot of trouble. There's some irony there I guess. Now that I've seen how the nobles live, I'm not sure I'd want to be one of them." She smoothed his sheet with her hands, and kept her eyes on her gloves. "But my father was a fair and good man, even if he couldn't be a real parent to me. He took me in, you see, when my mother, a maid, died of consumption when I was five or six. Of course he had his sons, so I had brothers. I was only half sister to them, as their mother had been noble, my father's rightful wife. She died long before I was old enough to remember her, giving birth to their second son about a year after I came into this world. I really had no legal right to be there, in their house, and the eldest son never let me forget it, but for some reason Father decided to keep me in his care after my mother perished. I worked as a serving girl and as sort of companion for his children." Fond memories. True, those years had been difficult, but easier by far than the rest of her life. Danica swallowed hard, and wished things had turned out different. Likely as not she would still be with the family in one way or another. *Likely you would be dead, girl.*

"I wasn't openly acknowledged; the family had some stature and they couldn't afford any scandal. They treated me well, though; I even received a bit of education while the other children got theirs. Like I said, I wasn't friendly with my older brother, but my younger brother and I got along very well. We were close in age, and both quite the troublemakers." She risked a glance at Tucker's face. The Raccoon's thoughtful expression indicated that he was apparently clearheaded despite his fever. Danica drew in a deep breath and wished they were alone, Fabrizio nowhere in earshot. "My younger brother and I had a bit of a fight one day. Not really odd, that. We used to fight all the time, just like most youngsters. Tussling, even a couple of serious ones that ended with him on his tail, nose bloodied - I was by far the tougher of the two of us. But this one.... I was nearly into my teens, and he as well." Danica sighed. At that age, children were confused about life, and prone to act on their emotions without thinking. She had been no exception. "Perhaps I was becoming a bit jealous of the attention my brothers received from Father, with no one in the family really interested in me except the younger one. Both boys excelled in nearly everything they tried, they were the heirs, they were their Father's sons.... I was just a bastard he'd taken in out of pity." As she spoke her old anger surged again and she began pacing the small room. Fabrizio skittered from her path to hide in the corner, evidently sensing the building tension in the room; like most stressful situations it frightened him. That must be it. Nothing more.

"The fight started simply enough - over a biscuit of all things. My brother snatched it from me as a joke while I was walking down a hall, and bolted it down. He was probably just laughing in good humor, but the look on his face seemed mocking to me, seemed cruel. My temper got the best of me, and we began wrestling. He pinned me down, still laughing, and I suddenly realized he was growing bigger than me, that he would soon get the better of me even in this. Something inside me snapped like an overdrawn bowstring, and the next thing I knew things were turned around. I was tearing at his face with my claws, and our father was dragging me off." Danica held the memory at arm's length. Detachment was the only defense that would allow her to finish this story. Tucker tossed the bloodied rag into the corner; Fabrizio started, his eyes jumping from her to the cloth and back again. Her throat grew thick despite her best efforts at control. "I tore up one of his eyes, scarred his face. There was no question whether I'd been trying to really, seriously injure him." Not even in my own mind. "The family was rich, so I suppose nothing came of the wounds; a good enough donation to the church probably gave him a full recovery, even the eye. But if my father hadn't pulled me away, I have no idea how much damage I would have caused. I might even have killed him."

The will to remain aloof began to crumble as Danica felt a betraying moisture fill her eyes. Tucker regarded her speculatively; she would have given good money to know what he was thinking. Fabrizio shifted back and forth, the sharp stink of fear rising from him. It was the only smell in the room, besides the blood; from Tucker there came nothing. "Father was...furious, to say the least. He didn't beat me, beyond the first rage when he was holding me back, but he accused me of betrayal, of jealousy, and hatred for my brother. It wasn't true, at all, but what could I say? He wanted me out of his house, but first," and her fists clenched spasmodically, "he called in a barber and had him pull my claws."

The voices of memory echoed in the dark places of her mind. 'You realize if I simply pull them, she may very well bleed to death, my Lord. Surgery is the usual method here.' The unfamiliar voice was terrible in its mildness.

'Pull them, but see that she survives. I care not how, so long as she lives. I will not have her death on my hands.' Her Father, and yet not. What kind of father would condemn his daughter to such a fate, speaking as coldly as though she were not in the room, pinned under the strong hands of one of the house guard, the very same guard who carried her on his shoulders around the courtyard.

'I could sear the wounds shut; there would be scarring, though.' The voice grew thoughtful as it presented a possible answer to the dilemma.

'Acceptable. Scarring is precisely the point here, barber.'

"He even had the barber burn the wounds shut with hot iron." Slowly she slid off one of the gloves, staring at the ruin of her index finger. A deeply pitted scar gazed back at her, puckered over, still terrible after all these years. So much pain for such a tiny space. The struggling, the agony, the heat, the burning. Tucker's words jarred her back to the present.

"Why did he pull your claws? You were out of the house, Danica." His voice was as flat as his eyes; there was little of Tuck there, only a cool, analytical stranger, searching for holes in her story. Realization struck like lightning. He doesn't believe me! Why? Abruptly Danica knew where this was leading; the cold knowledge settled over her bones, like snowflakes drifting down to cover a corpse. He's going to bring up Malik. He's leading to Fabrizio. The questions resembled Tucker's lengthy, convoluted strategies in Steel and Stone, but this time Danica could see no way out.

"'I want no danger for my sons from you, forever.' That's what he told me." The rest of her Father's pitiless speech to her, dimly remembered through the agony and self-hatred, crept back into her memories. 'Without claws, you will be seen as a criminal, or worse. None will believe you; none will hearken to you. You will have no claim, none at all, to my House. You will never be a threat to my sons.'

Father, how wrong you were.

"You're not telling me something."

Danica pinned him with her gaze, but this time it failed to fluster. "That's all I feel like telling you. Now, if you don't mind, I have business." She reached for Fabrizio and was leading him to the door when Tucker spoke again.

"I heard we have a Don's son again, Danica. Everyone in the city was talking about it on the way in. So who's your employer? The man sitting on the throne pretending to be Fabrizio?" The questions struck home like crossbow quarrels, and she stood still, eyes on the door, waiting for the rest, for the accusation. "Because we both know that the Fox shivering on your arm has to be the real Fabrizio. It can't be the one that's declared himself, coming out of nowhere. You already admitted as much on the trail who this one is. And why else go to so much trouble? Why else would he be cursed by Black magic, seeing that's how the Don was supposedly killed? Why would that Weasel be bringing him to the Avoirdupois? I'm guessing they'd pay a fair amount of gold to have the surviving Rinaldi heir in their hands. Speaking of money, after thinking for a bit I figured a moneylender like Tamurello wouldn't put up fifty gold aureals as a reward. So you're not working for him, either." The words came faster, now edged with emotion for the first time...anger. "And then there's Malik. He knew who you hunted, and he was after Fabrizio for the same people. Right? Bounty hunters." The Raccoon fairly spat the word.

Well, you wanted to cure him of his illusions, Danica thought in near hysteria, desperately trying to think of something, lie or truth, to buy her the time to think her way out of this predicament. It was her worst nightmare coming true. All along the Red Fox thought she could get everything: keep her friends, the gold, her own sense of self-worth. It was turning out to be an impossible juggling act, balls tumbling all around her.

A rustle came as Tucker shifted position, his tone slightly calmer. "You knew. You knew all along, and you weren't here to rescue him. You were here to bring him back, so he could be dealt with by this pretender." Slowly she turned to face him. His face still held its empty cast, his tone conversational and yet oddly lifeless. "Nice story about the claws, by the way; very well practiced. Who did you really betray? I may be no good with figures, but there's just too much here that doesn't add up."

Danica could hardly defend her past after Tucker's revelation of her motives concerning Fabrizio. In his eyes, her lack of claws simply reinforced her lack of honor. Whether her story was true or not had become academic. She stood mute under his accusations while he studied her with cool regard.

"You told me earlier, and I didn't believe you. It's all for the money, you said. I didn't want to see it. I wanted you to be special. Well, you are that...very special. You're worse than everyone else. You don't care at all, do you." A clinical observation, not a question. She wanted to cry out, deny his words, but how? "Malik was right - you're just like him. You use people, you treat everyone but your friends like dirt, you never do anything except for your own purposes, and you even lie to your supposed friends and manipulate them."

"That's not true," she burst out, unable to contain herself any longer. It couldn't be true! But try as she might, Danica could find no words with which to defend herself.

"No? Well, from what Malik said you didn't exactly put yourself on the line to save a couple of children. But you did use their deaths to get rid of him. You lied to me from the start. You were willing to jerk me and Delaney around by our noses just to keep us from figuring out what kind of person you were. You even pulled us into your little scheme."

"I didn't know at the time," Danica whispered.

Tucker snorted. "Sure, Danica. Whatever you say. And then you're bringing back this Fabrizio. Even if you 'didn't know at the time', we figured it out on the trail, so you knew exactly what you were bringing him back to. Whether you stick a blade in him yourself, or hand him over to the hooded one with the axe, murder is murder, Danica. And he isn't guilty of anything but having noble blood running in his veins."

Murder is murder. The phrase was familiar, heard recently, and when the bounty hunter realized where, her hands began to shake. Murder is murder...her own words. Danica swayed on her feet, and Fabrizio crawled forward to wrap his fingers around her gloved fist, murmuring incoherently in soft, worried tones.

Tucker studied his fingers sadly, and rubbed a missed spot of crimson from one with the sheets. "I even killed for you." His face twisted for an instant. "Delaney's right about me. Such a damned fool!" Danica reached out towards her friend, caught by his pain, but jerked her hand back, unwilling to suffer the rejection she knew would follow her touch. Tucker stared at his own hands for a few moments longer, unwilling to look at her, before sighing deeply and continuing in the same barren tone. "I'm thinking you ought not come around here anymore. I don't really want to see your face, and I figure Delaney will feel the same once I tell him. Also Porter and Desmond. Especially Desmond, you know how he is. Or maybe you don't. Maybe you don't really know any of us."

"You wouldn't," Danica whispered. He couldn't strip away all of her friends. Bad enough she was losing him, but all of them? Malik, is this what you felt when I took away Mo-gei? But unlike Malik, there was no one to conveniently blame but herself.

Tucker sucked in a deep breath, wincing at the pull in his chest. "DELANEY!" he bellowed, the shout making her cringe and driving Fabrizio back into the corner in a whimpering huddle. She held up her hands, trying to placate the Raccoon, but he drew in another breath , glaring at her.

"All right! I'm leaving!" The words spilled out like the blood from Malik's throat, leaving her equally hollow. I can't believe it. This can't be happening! A trickle of anger rushed in to fill the void. "You don't have a clue what you're talking about, Tucker," she hissed, grabbing Fabrizio by the wrist and dragging him away from the supine Raccoon. "You're a cursed thief; you steal. You've no call to be making moral judgments on other people!" There must be something to say to wipe that disgust from his eyes, to hurt him as he had hurt her. "You're nothing but a poor gutter rat. You don't know what I've been through. Don't you dare judge me!"

"I grew up in this shit-heap, Danica," he returned icily, gesturing out the broken-shuttered window at Old Town. "Me and my sister both. We didn't even have Delaney until we were ten or eleven, so spare me the sob story. My sister's in the church now, and I don't drag innocent people to their deaths for money. How about that? Maybe we make our own choices." Tucker waited for her reply, but all she could do was stand mute, overcome with rage and shame, keeping Fabrizio's wrist in her hand. In truth, the Red Fox was unable to think of a single argument to refute his disgusted appraisal. The Raccoon shrugged, turning away to stare through his mask out the window. "Get your tail out of my room."

Danica slowly gathered up her things from the floor as Tucker continued to stare at the slowing rainfall. With each item she collected, she paused to check and see if he was watching her. Never once did his expression change. When she picked up her full pack, the bounty hunter stood for several heartbeats, staring at the burglar, willing him to turn, to smile, to forgive her, even to rail at her again. Anything.

Eventually she left. There was nothing else to do.

                              *   *   *

Danica had little difficulty bringing Fabrizio through the city unrecognized; the people knew where their ruler was, and certainly he would not be found cowering in torn peasant's clothes in the slowing drizzle with the likes of her. At first the bounty hunter steered her charge in the direction of the Rinaldi palace. With a mind brimming full of whirling questions, accusations, and regrets, she operated purely on instinct. Finish the job. Mo-gei's words cut through the confusion, lending a certain stability to her actions. It really was the right thing to do; despite her emotional turmoil Danica held onto that spar like a drowning woman. No need to make a decision, just remember your teaching. Finish the job.

Unfortunately, the massive Rinaldi palace gates were securely closed, a massive black iron denial. No one answered her hammering on the smaller door in the gate. She stared at Fabrizio worriedly as he threw back his hood and gaped at the massive iron doors. Slowly the cursed noble ran his hand over the worked metal, an expression of faint wonder growing on his face. He's probably never seen those gates closed to him before. The thought struck a chord of empathy in Danica. Her Father, her mentor, now her friends. Everyone she had cared for was taken from her, and now the same was happening to Fabrizio.

Or did I throw them away, rather than lose them?

"It's still locked up," came a familiar voice.

Danica carefully replaced the hood over Fabrizio's head before turning to face the Skunk. It was the same one as before, returning from rounds along the wall. This time he looked considerably more miserable, for though the Rinaldi issued all of the Guard heavy oiled cloaks, the damp still crept in under the cloak. Standing out here in the wet would be foul duty indeed. "Where's your friend?"

Snorting, the Skunk shook his sopping head. "Sick. Rotten bugger's prob'ly sitting himself down in front of a fire with an ale."

"I heard Fabrizio was back." At his name the Grey Fox turned his cloaked head; thankfully, that was all, and the Skunk noticed nothing untoward.

"Well, he's back, but not here." The Guard looked at her hopefully. Danica sighed and dug into her purse, flipping him two silver denarii. He caught them out of the air, nearly bobbling one. "That's it?"

"No one to share it with, this time," she replied.

The guard brightened. "True." Scratching his ear, he thought for an instant, evidently sorting out the facts in his head. Danica could appreciate that; much better to pay for clear, concise information than the babblings of an idiot. "Seems that there's some money owed, and the palace and lands is part of the assurance. The heir isn't allowed in until it's all settled. Also, I hear there's word of a purification being held soon by the Church on the Keep itself." He quickly made the sign to ward off the evil eye. "Black magic killed the Don and his son. So they say."

Considering this information, Danica barely restrained a laugh despite her despondent mood. Money owed? Truly the nobility was falling on hard times in Triskellion if a commoner could dictate terms. And Black magic? Whenever someone of importance died it was always Black magic - and for once, the rumors were correct. "Where's he staying now?"

"Um, I'm not sure," he said, flashing an apologetic smile. When the bounty hunter started digging in her purse again, the Skunk waved his hands in front of her, startling Fabrizio into leaping back behind her with a sharp cry. "No, no, no, no! I really don't know! Just some inn. New Town."

"Fair enough." Taking Fabrizio gently by the wrist, Danica began to lead him from the gates. The mad Fox craned his neck as they walked, staring over his shoulder at the guard, the crumbling walls, and the ancient, black metal barrier. A faint sound escaped his throat. Perhaps a whimper of loss, or more likely fear. Perhaps, Danica imagined, it was even resignation.

Over a hundred paces away from the gates the realization that she never thanked the Skunk sank in. 'You use people. You treat everyone but your friends like dirt.' Tucker's "No," Danica whispered, "I'm not like that." Fabrizio stared curiously as she turned, hunting for the guard in the rain.

He was already gone on his rounds.

*   *   *

Three Spears Inn, Danica thought as she trudged through the rain, keeping her eye out for unwelcome encounters. The Otter will want the fake to stay away from the Merchant's Guild until he's settled in and unassailable - they're the most likely to notice something wrong. The merchants also had both the power and the motive to upset the Pretender's plans; long chafing under the rule of the nobility, the Merchant's Guild held a great deal of influence in Triskellion. To finally divest themselves of the ruling yoke, false or true, would be the culmination of many of their members' dreams. The Skunk's right. He won't be staying with any merchants, even if they offer. He needs a private place, somewhere he can stay out of reach...the best inn in the city.

Until they finally passed through the gates into New Town, Danica felt on razor's edge, nerves trembling with tension. At any instant Delaney or another of her friends could step out of the rain, demanding their own explanation. To go through that again would kill her; better to leave and never return. Better to trust only in herself.

Despite the gently hissing rain, a fair sized crowd had gathered outside the Inn's estate, held off by the massive stone walls. Danica sighed, and gently pulled the terrified Fabrizio away; he feared they would be pushing through the inn's besiegers and began trembling immediately. "We'll come back later." The grateful look he gave her deepened the wound cut by Tucker's words. I have nothing else now but myself. Remember that. She ruffled his fur, running gloved fingers thoughtfully along his cheekbone again. "Come on. We'll find somewhere quiet for the afternoon." There was no reason to torment the poor mendicant.

"D..dd...dd," he agreed, stuttering and nodding foolishly in relief. It was by far the most articulate speech he had yet uttered. Beyond his brief reverie at the Keep's gates he still demonstrated no signs of familiarity with the city, as lost as a total stranger. For an instant doubt touched the Red Fox; what if somehow she were wrong, what if this was not Fabrizio and they were caught up in the playing out of a completely different plot? She pulled off a glove and put her hand on the side of his face, turning him towards her to look in his eyes. There was nothing of intelligence to be seen, no more than a riding dray, but Danica was sure this was the Rinaldi heir. No doubt at all.

The two weary Foxes spent the day on the steps of the Cathedrale De Temoin, across the Market Square from the Three Spears. The enormous edifice, all spires, towers, and stained glass, was the end of many a pilgrimage to Triskellion for the purpose of paying homage to the martyrdom of Heloise. The heart of the Church of S'allumer, the awesome building housed a legion of clergy, a massive library second to none, and the only fully comprehensive school of Theurgy in existence. Dedicated to the worship of the True Faith, the Cathedrale was a shining light on the occasionally shadowed island of Calabria. At the moment, though, the only part of it Danica found herself interested in was the marble stairs. They served to keep her out of the muddy puddles and also provided a good vantage point from which to observe the Three Spears Inn, across the marketplace.

The rain tapered off quickly and Fabrizio, features shadowed by Danica's cloak, sat watching the small, scavenging lizards scampering about the massive edifice of stone and stained glass. From high on the steps Danica studied the commotion at the inn over the heads and stalls of the market crowd. Even at this distance she could identify some of the more prominent members of the Triskellion Guilds: several leaders of the Merchant's Guild, a high ranker in the Goldsmith's Guild (for whom she had done work in the past, tracking down a member who absconded with some of the raw materials); even an uncomfortable looking Master of the recently formed Sailor's Guild, his fashionable but well-worn clothing looking quite out of place amongst all of the finery. All of them left soon after their arrivals, identical disgruntled expressions souring their widely different faces. So, the Otter isn't taking any chances with his protégé.

Even the few visitors from the clergy were sent out after a perfunctory visit. Danica listened in on a conversation between two of them entering the Cathedrale; it seemed the Don-to-be would undergo a ritual of purification, in order to cleanse him of any taint of the foul magicks that took the life of his father and brother. The Priests seemed convinced it should be soon, for 'the peril to his soul may be great'. Danica stole a look at Fabrizio, chortling with childlike delight at the antics of the lizards.

Too late, Fathers.

The bounty hunter almost called out to them as they passed, but held her tongue. Danica could not begin to explain the urge. Above all else in her mind, confusion reigned supreme. It clouded her decisions, making her unable to commit to the simplest action beyond blindly following her original plan.

The situation was hardly clear, and with her first real opportunity to think since this fiasco had begun, Danica turned what she knew over and over in her head, looking for the thread to untangle the whole affair. Assuming the Otter's first encounter with the real Fabrizio was at Tamurello's, why had he not simply acted then against the Weasel? He would have been facing an unknown Wizard and her henchmen, alone. Plus he would hardly wish to call more attention to the real heir - it might result in his plans being exposed. Then why had he waited such a long time before unleashing hunters to go after the group? Despite what her employer had said, Danica suspected she was the first on the scene; with the Wizard and her captive not terribly difficult to trace, Danica felt certain that the first competent

hunter would have discovered them. Malik simply took the easiest route, following an already established pursuit. Loyalty was the issue there; he needed out-of-towners, hunters known to have no true affiliation to Triskellion. He couldn't risk some last vestige of allegiance to the Rinaldi pushing the hunters to save the rightful heir should they recognize the Grey Fox as such. Perhaps they might even become rivals to his plans. And the Otter would know Fabrizio could not possibly sway outlanders in his current state; with the chance meeting, even should the Pretender's advisor not be of the esoteric Green and Purple College, the mind-delvers and dream-spinners, a few moments in the same room with the madman would serve to reassure the mage of the real Fabrizio's incompetence. He sent out riders looking for hunters immediately; being in Three Rivers, I just happened to be closest.

Danica's eyes fell on Fabrizio, sitting one step below her, toying with the edge of her cloak. Time to think suddenly proved to be curse. Fifty gold aureals was a fair bit of money, but was it enough to justify turning an innocent over to his murderers? He's cursed; his mind's gone. It'll be a blessing. The rationalization fell flat in the hollowness in her gut. What in the name of the Blessed Light of Truth and Beauty am I doing? "Murder is murder," she whispered. I can't do this!

A darker thought took hold, pushing away the guilt. Oh, come on Danica; Tucker was right, and this certainly would not be the first time you've done something questionable. When times were tough, you hunted slaves and brought them back to their owners for the reward. You put yourself before everyone. It's the only way to survive. The two sides of her mind fought viciously, no quarter given. There's so much gold there - his mind's gone anyway. He isn't even Fabrizio de Rinaldi anymore! It was a certainty that sooner or later someone with no scruples would find the poor lunatic. There was no possible way she could bring him along wherever she went, protect him. Leaving him in a hostel run by the church would be signing his death warrant. At least this way she could benefit from the gold. Sure Danica; run your fingers through the bloody gold. Only Mo-gei's teaching kept coming back clearly. The damned contract.. Caught in her indecision, Danica sat, wrestling with inertia as the day wore on.

It turned out to feel like quite a long time, Danica's fight with Tucker at the Crested Mastiff intruding over and over again. Try as she might, it was impossible for the Fox to find a better way this could have turned out. You made your choice; you can't go back. Live with it. Despite all attempts to convince herself otherwise, the bounty hunter still held a desperate hope that something, anything, could be salvaged. Perhaps Tucker would listen to reason. Perhaps the others would believe her over him if she lied. Perhaps, perhaps, perhaps....

And what of Fabrizio?

When the sun finally began to dip below the rooftops, Danica stood and brushed off her trousers. It was time; most of the doubts had vanished under sharp-edged purpose. Just keep moving; everything will work out if you just get moving. "Come on, 'Rizio," she muttered automatically. The mad Fox started, head snapping around, eyes widening before he realized who spoke. Obediently, the noble struggled to his swollen feet and stood, eyes darting to and fro, waiting for her command. Danica wanted to shake him. Run! Run away, fool! Instead, she took his hand to lead him through the crowd.

The stony walls of the Three Spears stood only just above head-height on a tall Bear, not much compared with the Rinaldi Keep, but they sufficed quite well to accomplish their primary purpose - privacy. The miniature fortifications kept out the casual bystander, the occasional thief. More persistent invaders were held at bay by the inn's reputation for hiring very large, very angry guards. The Three Spears' continued profit depended on its ability to keep the customers happy, and one service every one of them paid out silver for was a curtain to draw against the world outside. Those hired to keep that curtain closed took their duties very seriously.

Thus Danica found it odd they were stopped at the massive front doors by one of the Triskellion Guard. The Red Fox looked him up and down disdainfully. The heavyset Armadillo glared at her, leaning forward myopically to get a better look through the bars of the gate. "I don't care if you're Heloise herself...," he began, but Danica cut him off with a single comment.

"The Anathasian."

The guard's mouth snapped shut for an instant, but only that. "So you've heard something. You're going to have to do better than that." Crossing huge arms in front of his chest, the thick-set creature frowned at her sourly. "I'm not running all the way to the back with nothing more to go on."

"Tell the Anathasian Danica has a package for him." She put as much annoyance as possible into the phrase. "If he doesn't want it, I can always find someone else to hand it to."

The guard grunted and turned away, motioning to a nearby Wolverine in the same livery to take his place. As the armor-plated behemoth swaggered off he took a quick glance over his shoulder; from where she stood, the bounty hunter could see fear flash in his nearsighted eyes. Good. Danica smiled; better to have him afraid of her.

"You treat everyone but your friends like dirt."

The smile faded. Fabrizio whined and tugged at her hand. She leaned back against the wall and tried to take a deep breath; it came out in a shuddering moan.

Danica knew all about those who treated people like objects to be used, then thrown away. Nearly all of her life she had hunted them. Killed them. And now the Fox could see it, so plainly. Once again, Tucker was correct. She took, took, and took some more, never returning anything. Malik had seen it as well; the twisted Coyote recognized a kindred soul, and sought to destroy it. She wondered at his friendship with Mo-gei, his desperate loyalty despite their totally different natures. Look who I have for friends. Tucker, Delaney, even Desmond and Porter. Do we all yearn for something better? Do we all hate ourselves so much?

Bounty hunting was all she knew: Use a weapon, hunt a person for money. Setting up shop somewhere as a merchant was a possibility; no doubt she would shortly thereafter die of starvation. Danica almost laughed at the idea. Living in

102

poverty isn't my idea of life. Death would be preferable, and since that thought hardly appealed... "Sorry 'Rizio-Fabrizio," she finished, mentally cursing her slip. With an effort she put some mental distance between them. "Looks like you lose. Again."

Fabrizio snarled nervously, seeming in reply, but then Danica made out faint noises approaching. It was the guard returning. Frantically, involuntarily, her mind hunted furiously, looking for a way to make something better out of this situation, some trick by which she could get what she wished without losing any more. I've already lost my friends - I can't afford to lose anything else! If she ran with Fabrizio, she burdened herself with a cursed fool and broke her contract as a hunter. Word would get out and there would be no more lucrative job offers coming her way, ever again. Danica would live out her life on small rewards found in even smaller towns, staying one step ahead of her former peers, themselves hired by her furious former employer to hunt her down. And she would never be able to release Fabrizio; anyone to whom she handed him could be found eventually, and they both would die. Nowhere to run, and impossible odds to fight.

Better for them both if it ended now, cleanly and easily.

Easily for whom, Danica?

The Armadillo yanked open the gates in the wall, staggering in his haste to reach her. "Ahhh, the Lord Fabrizio's advisor will see you now," he gasped. Danica nodded cooly, ears picking up the sound of heavy, booted feet on the walkway inside the gate. She peered past the gatekeeper's bulk and made out two forms, one short and whip-thin, the other dwarfing the guard in height and mass. "These men," the Armadillo finished, "will be escorting you. And your friend." He tried a bow; it was truly pathetic, but Danica felt a moment's pity for him and nodded curtly before taking Fabrizio, her Fabrizio, by the elbow. She led him carefully around the huge, wheezing figure to walk towards the two silhouettes awaiting them on the path to the Inn.

Scant few heartbeats later found them hurried along cobbled pathways on the side of the inn towards the Three Spears' second guest building. Built of white marble in the rear of the modest estate, its materials imported at a tremendous cost from the Doloreaux, the guest suite was a smaller structure, resembling nothing less than a nobleman's summer cottage or small manor house. An expensive coup for the Three Spears, the building contained but one set of rooms, opulently furnished and catering only to the nobility or the more affluent of the merchants; few others could afford its exorbitant prices. The benefits of the suite could be well worth the cost; it was the perfect place for visiting merchants to conduct business outside of the guild halls, and for nobility of the other Great Houses to rest themselves in comfort with their retinue when visiting Triskellion: luxurious, elegant, spacious and above all, private.

The two guards ushering her into the room where the Otter awaited them were a cold and dangerous sort. Quite a pair they struck as well: a massive Rhinoceros in rusty, heavy mail and a vicious-eyed Rat in bright scale armor, his hand light on a rapier hilt. The air about them hung heavily with the stench of sudden violence.

Hired killers both; one did not spend so much time hunting the like without being
to recognize them by sight and scent. Not members of the Watch at all, the Fox
surmised.

For an instant Danica pondered the rather disturbing possibility that her silence
would be bought with blood rather than gold, but she dismissed the thought. She
would be a fool to speak out against the nobility; the Otter would likewise be a fool
if he murdered every successful employee. Either treachery was bad business and,
should word get out, could ruin one's reputation. If Danica spoke against her
employer, right or wrong, she would be hard pressed to find work outside hunting
for publicly denounced criminals. Similarly, if the mage had her killed and that fact
slipped into the rumor mill, he would find it most difficult to hire competent
people to do her kind of work.

The room itself was likely the best the Three Spears had to offer, and Danica let
her eyes roam freely as their little group entered. The bounty hunter had never
actually been inside this inn before, nor another of comparable class since her
childhood. Even in this simple meeting area the marble walls were colored with
hanging silks in a bewildering array of hues and tapestries crafted in intricate detail
depicting the martyrdom of Heloise, while a foreign rug of an elegant, handwoven
design warmed the floor. Dark wooden furniture, heavily carved, lent an air of
solemnity to the chamber, complementing its purpose. A huge rectangular table
dominated the room. It could seat several people comfortably, or two could sit
across from one another and still be close enough to discuss private affairs in hushed
voices. Naturally a small buffet stood against the far wall, carven to match the
furniture and sporting several crystal decanters. The Otter turned from one as they
entered, holding a small snifter in his paw. She could see the liquid within shimmer
slightly as if his wrist trembled. A little nervous, are we?

Chapter Ten

"Thank the ancients," the Wizard whispered as Danica stepped through the room up to the table, Fabrizio practically on her heels to avoid the steely-eyed Rhino. To the other side, the Rat grinned happily at the display of fear. "You have him! I...the resemblance is uncanny, is it not?"

Whatever the greeting Danica expected, babbling was not it. The last time she had seen the Otter he was the picture of condescending superiority, a towering column of arrogance swathed in a black leather cloak. He's strung tighter than a wounded Shrew, she realized. With all of the visits from the people of power, and without the true heir safely eliminated, the degree of stress on the Otter must be immense. The Fox thought she actually liked him better this way. It came to her that the true Pretender was nowhere to be seen. Well, well; so it is the Wizard masterminding this whole deal. Or at the very least, he's fronting it for another. I wonder, just where does his magical power come from? Not an Elementalist; he's far too subtle. Green and Purple College? Logically there would be a mind-twister behind this in order to better control the heir and deflect any suspicion.

"No problem," she replied carelessly, her tone belying the sick roiling of her stomach. Almost finished with this nightmare, she could soon put it behind her. She could walk away and start over, forget this ever happened. Somehow. "Do you have the payment?"

Of course he did, opening the buffet and snatching out the bulging purse, hands still a-tremble. Despite his apparent tension, a faint smile hovered at the corners of his lips. The stench of fear in the air subsided somewhat as Danica took the leather satchel, far heavier than a bag of denarii. Here it was: the gold. It would suffice to keep her alive and in good health for a very long time. Perhaps it was even enough to buy her some peace. Peace like Mo-gei had near the end, Danica? She weighed it in her hand, opening the purse to verify the contents, then dropped it to the table. The Otter tensed, shifting his weight, but relaxed as the bounty hunter slipped off her pack, opening it to carefully place the oh, so heavy gold within.

She was actually doing it, actually following through. Something inside still found itself surprised. After her ruminations on the stairs of the Cathedrale, Danica half expected her hand to throw back the bag of its own accord. Inertia, again, was carrying her through. Already here, having come this far, she found herself again unable to back out . Not for a madman, or for what remained of her morals.

She simply could not see any other way.

The massive Rhinoceros caught Fabrizio by one arm; he pulled back violently, staring at her mutely in shock. Danica returned the gaze, flat faced, mind empty and stomach quiet now. With a quick yank the Rhino pulled the Grey Fox away, dragging him towards the rear of the room. For an instant the cursed noble complied, then exploded into violent motion, struggling and snarling, desperately trying to free his arm from the iron grip. The bitter stink of terror filled the room as the Rhino fought with the Fox, the Rat stepping forward to lend assistance; in his

madness, Fabrizio put up quite a bit of resistance.. "D...dddd ...dd...," he
stammered, tears welling in his eyes as the two soldiers overpowered him.

Danica watched, dully. A dreamlike lassitude settled over her, and in an odd
way a sense of relief. She had to stand by her decision now, good or bad.

"I admit, you appeared a trifle wild - eyed when you came in," the Otter muttered
genially, heading back to the sideboard for another drink, completely dismissing the
frantic struggles of his captive as unimportant. "It almost seemed as if you were
considering refusing your reward." Pouring another half glass, he swirled it
carefully, studying how the amber liquid clung to the side when the motion ceased.
It seemed that with the completion of the contract the Wizard had regained his
usual aplomb, ruffled fur soothed and tension leeched away.

The Rat drove a fist into Fabrizio's gut; he doubled over, sagging in the Rhino's
grasp, arms instantly pinioned by the massive hands. All fight began to drain out of
the Fox now; despite the curse no doubt screaming in his mind to escape,
exhaustion and unceasing fear were crippling his will to struggle.

"Lystragones? What's going on?"

The Otter rose smoothly to his feet, directing his attention towards the door
leading into the bedchambers. A Grey Fox stood there, swathed in a brocade
dressing gown and rubbing his eyes sleepily. There was indeed an uncanny
resemblance between him and Fabrizio, but up close Danica could make out the
slight differences distinguishing one from the other. Ironically they were more
similar in looks now than they would have been before the hunt; days on the run,
cursed with fear, had taken their toll on Fabrizio, and he had lost weight, growing
slimmer. The Pretender's face, slightly sharper than it should be, now matched the
original's almost perfectly. The similarity was so very close, Danica thought, that it
would fool anyone not bothering to look for differences although perhaps not
someone who knew Fabrizio intimately. And they're all dead now, she thought
sadly, and with a certain hint of irony. All of them.

"It is nothing, my Lord. Please, retire to your rooms," the Otter began to suggest,
but the Pretender cut him off with a shocked cry.

"That's him, isn't it? That's the one you told me about, Lystragones! The peasant
Imposter!" He stepped up to the trio, staring at Fabrizio thrashing weakly in the
arms of the Rhinoceros. "In truth, he appears only vaguely similar to myself."
Danica fought to keep back a snort of annoyance. "So, fellow, now do you see your
reward for trying to steal the throne?" His eyes glittered with mean-spirited
satisfaction. "Anything to say, hmmm?" Fabrizio merely whined and continued his
futile struggles. "Light, the fellow's witless," the Pretender exclaimed angrily,
rounding on the Wizard. Suddenly he let out a bark of harsh laughter. "They
would supplant me with this ragamuffin? Idiots! Whoever they are; anyone with
half a brain would see through this pathetic plot in an instant!"

You're one to talk about half a brain, Danica thought. The imposter definitely
believed he actually was Fabrizio - that settled the question as to what college the
Wizard belonged. Green and Purple, no doubt at all.

"Yes, my lord," muttered the Otter quietly. "We will discover the identities of those behind this scheme, and bring them to justice. Your justice," he amended unctuously, but Danica saw the light of derision flash briefly in his hooded eyes.

Unfortunately the Grey Fox missed it completely, and preened under what he took for flattery. Then his eyes fell on Danica. "Well well," he leered salaciously. "What have we here?" When Danica merely stared back impassively, without the usual simpering the Pretender no doubt expected from women, the foppish puppet took a closer sniff and his snout wrinkled in disgust. "Another one of your mercenaries, Lystragones?"

"Hardly, my Lord." The bounty hunter felt the cut of the Otter's offhanded insult. "She is, in fact, the hunter to whom we owe thanks for capturing this traitor." Fabrizio snarled, and in his fear, tried to bite the Rat, but the Rhino hammered him back into the wall hard enough to drive the breath from his lungs. Wincing delicately, the Pretender kept his attention on Danica.

"She stinks of blood and burned meat. For the love of Light, Wizard," he whined, "heal her. I can hardly bear the stench."

"As you command, my Lord," the Otter breathed with a faint edge to his voice. He reached out, nose wrinkling with disgust, and touched Danica's shoulder lightly. Danica nearly stepped back, wary and disliking, on principle, to have magic cast upon her, but a ripple of pain from her scorched legs helped keep her in place. It infuriated her that she should be dealt with like a beast of burden or a piece of furniture. Or a slave. A torrent of syllables flew from the Wizard's lips, and his pupils dilated sharply as the magic rippled forth. It felt like cool rain, passing down over her body and washing away the dirt and pain. Having been on the receiving end of Theurgy in the past, Danica recognized it as a very minor healing spell; evidently the Otter was loathe to waste any more of his precious power on her. While it certainly helped the pain and eased the stiffness in her legs, the spell did nothing for her frustrated thoughts.

Is this the sort of person I'll be dealing with forever? Someone who despises me, or thinks of me as nothing more than a pair of hands, a tool? Suddenly it made sense to Danica why Malik cared so much about his friendship with Mo-gei, why Mo-gei had been so horrified at the truth about the Coyote. Why it hurt so terribly much to lose her own friends, to feel so alone.

When dealing with these people day in, day out, one would be very, very thankful for what friends they had, friends who cared for who one was, not what one could do for them. Strange she failed to realize this until too late, until all of her friends were gone.

The Pretender dabbed his nose with a perfumed handkerchief, losing interest in Danica. "Well, what shall we do with this one? A public execution perhaps?"

"No! Rather, my Lord," the Otter continued more quietly when the pretender spun to face him, eyes wide with shock, "I only fear for your position. No one need hear of this false Fabrizio. There would be whispers, discussions of this in houses low, high, and Great. Better the masses see only the truth we present to them." The irony sickened Danica, but the annoyance faded from the Grey Fox's face, replaced by a worried cast.

"True, true," he muttered, glancing at the guards speculatively. The unwholesome light of paranoia flowered in his eyes. "We must be very careful whom we trust. Very well; what would you suggest?"

"A silent death, here and now, my Lord. The servants are bribed, and this edifice is secure. A trip to the privy, his throat slit, and the body removed for disposal elsewhere." Danica gritted her teeth, choking back her feelings.

"Very good." The Pretender sighed with satisfaction. "Then perhaps I can get some sleep. Deal with it," he snapped at the guards. The Rat bowed, muttering something unhealthy under his breath the Pretender did not catch. He turned to the Rhino just in time to get a piece of one ear taken cleanly off by a snap of bright fangs as Fabrizio suddenly erupted into one last furious effort to free himself.

By the madman's glazed eyes and unfocused thrashing, Danica could see it had been an accident, but the Rat, putting one hand to his ear, let out a enraged shout. His hand shot out, a blur in the air. Danica blinked in surprise. The movement was so quick she missed its impact. Fabrizio's head jerked to the side, bright blood seeping through the fur of his right cheek, sliced raggedly by the Rat's claws. Cursing, the ruffian whipped out a dagger, but froze at a command from the Otter. "Nothere." The Wizard punctuated his words with a nod in the direction of the wide-eyed Pretender. Fairly shaking with fury, the Rat swung toward the robed Grey Fox and gave another short bow.

"Beggin' your pardon, m'Lord."

Danica could only stare, captivated by the blood seeping into the fur of Fabrizio's face.

Slowly the cursed noble brought his head up, breathing heavily. Turned about during the struggle, he now faced Danica. The Rhino's horned, grinning face stared at her from behind his captive's shoulder as the stunned, trapped madman caught her with his gaze. A desperate entreaty shone there for her and her alone. Despite their past, despite the curse, despite the bounty hunter's betrayal, Fabrizio reached out to the person Danica realized he still recognized as the one to whom he always turned for help. "D...ddddd...d...d," the Grey Fox wheezed in his stumbling voice, then drew in an anguished breath, expelling it in an agonized scream. Just as he had, years ago, when the night terrors took hold and he needed her to keep them away.

"DAAANNNIII!"

The heavy blade, jerked from its sheath and pitched underhand in one single, violent motion, slid past her brother's ear, clearing it by only a finger's breadth. Her fingers remained in the air, leveled at the huge man's throat; a foot of steel hammered precisely where she had aimed it. Fabrizio, released, shoved the Rat aside and ducked under the table, howling in terror. Roaring, the Rhino spat crimson as he reached to pull the Chevernaise knife from his neck. Danica beat him to it, stepping in to tear the weapon free in a sideways rip, opening the arteries. One! Blood fanned the walls, the mercenary crumpled, and she shifted to face the Rat, her knife deflecting one, two, three thrusts before she gained enough room to pull steel and sweep the air in a tight, shining arc that forced him back. For an instant the tips of their swords danced against each other; then he thrust again and she barely avoided it, losing fur. His speed with the rapier would make a mockery of most opponents, and a corpse.

Out of the corner of her eye Danica was aware of the Otter moving quickly to put distance between them. Heloise! Two at once, now! Finally reacting, the Pretender eerily mimicked the real Fabrizio by screaming in horror, albeit in falsetto, then retreated back into the bedroom, slamming the door behind him. A rattle of furniture being piled against the barrier echoed an instant later.

"Nice sword," whispered the Rat, blood dripping from his bitten ear. "I bet you think you're fast." He lunged, terribly swift on the point, but she slid the attack away, up her blade and to the side. Partly blocked, his returning draw cut opened her shoulder, and before Danica could riposte the Rat snapped back at the ready. "Ain't nobody quicker than me, girl." Another thrust, and she parried with a whip of her blade that cut the point up under the end of his jaw. When he jerked back, surprised, she flicked the razor tip and bounced it off his forehead. Blood now flowed from both his sliced jaw and the scalp wound. "You-!" Enraged, he wiped his forehead and lunged, full extension. Two. Danica sidestepped smoothly and watched his eyes widen in sudden realization. She took the wrist, thigh, then throat, and whirled to face the Wizard.

The two mercenaries served their purpose; on the other side of the table now, the Otter was across the room with staff raised with a spell no doubt at the ready. Danica twisted her shoulders, beginning the underhanded throw to send the knife hurtling into the Otter's chest. Instead, she found herself falling into his shadowed eyes, grown huge and fiery, drinking in her mind and spirit and leaving her void and numbed. She stumbled, off balance but not falling, limbs growing dull and heavy, body sinking into a syrupy torpor. 'Rizio...I'm sorry. Some part of her thoughts, still darting about wildly within the confines of her mind, cursed her own stupidity. Stupid to go back on a contract. Stupid to come this far and then attack her employer in his own room, full of his own people. Above all, stupid to throw her brother to the Mastiffs, even after so many years apart. Stupid and sickeningly, unforgivably wrong. 'I don't drag innocent people to their deaths for money.' Tucker's words, but how much hotter would his scorn have burned knowing who 'Rizio had been to her?

Had been...for with her caught under the icy, mind-numbing web of the Mage's spell, they were both dead.

The Otter stepped quickly around the jerking body of the dying Rat and shot a faintly repulsed glance at the corpse of the Rhino. "Well. That could have gone better," he muttered absently. "Why did you not simply complete your contract?" His tone of voice was one of a disappointed uncle, conversing with a niece caught stealing pies from a baker. Bending swiftly, he jerked a dagger from the horned mercenary's mammoth boot. "Why pick now, of all times, to develop a conscience?"

109

The Otter moved closer, his queries obviously rhetorical. "Or did someone else pay you more, perhaps, to kill me? Most foolish." From the way he held the weapon, there was no question he planned on using it. "Though I don't know who that would be. Well, speak! You might yet walk away from this little blunder." It was an utterly transparent lie; only a fool would release her now. Danica desperately fought the spell holding her in place, draining the strength from her limbs.

"My brother," she whispered back hopelessly, trying to buy time again but for once with the truth. "You said there were Rinaldi bastards. You were right." Stopping in his advance, the stunned Mage gaped at her. The explanation certainly could not have been what he expected. "Couldn't do it. Almost, but...." A change of heart, coming far, far too late for any possible redemption. Danica's mind raged against its magic prison. If she could only gain a few more heartbeats, she felt the spell might shatter. Unfortunately its master was well aware of this; the dagger came up as he stepped close.

"An illuminating conversation," he purred, recovering his aplomb, "but whether this is simply your own insanity or the truth, I'm afraid the rest of your revelations will have to wait. Forever." Gripping her shoulder the wizard raised the small, sharp edge to her throat with a slight shudder of distaste. The blade trembled for an instant, then grew steady.

A heartbeat from making the cut the wizard's eyes flew wide and he shrieked, lurching back and flailing wildly. Fabrizio, snarling hideously, had lunged forward from under the table and fastened teeth into the Otter's calf. "You fiend!" the Wizard screamed in pain and surprise. Twice delivered in one day by another, and still in grip of the spell, Danica could only watch, praying, as they grappled, murderous snarls rising from the savage struggle. Slashing down with the dagger, the Otter cut clumsily along her brother's arm. The mad Fox wailed as he fell back, the curse of terror once again clouding his eyes.

Danica's mind blazed, as she remembered lullabies sung in the dark to her brother whimpering under the demon's talons of a nightmare. Deeply buried shame, her brother's ruined face and eye, added fuel to the flames. The mystic power of the glacial shackles on her body and mind melted in the furnace of her fury. The Otter swung back towards her, sensing that the spell was failing, desperately reaching out with the short dagger. Cold steel ran along her cheek, missing her throat by a hand's breadth. Her left arm, weighted with short, heavy steel, thrust forward.

She cratered him.

For an instant they froze, the bounty hunter and the Wizard, linked by a razor-edged length of steel. Then Danica twisted her wrist and thrust the blade down. The Otter hit the ground howling, hands fighting, but failing, to keep the blood from spilling out. Danica stepped back and raised the point of her sword up under his sobbing mouth. A flare of light erupted from the Mage's wound at that instant; a hung spell of some sort, set for what contingency she knew not. Nothing overt occurred, and she relaxed minutely, the tip of Mo-gei's sword rock steady, belying her wobbling knees.

Despite the danger in which she now stood, Danica felt suddenly possessed by a sensation of terrible freedom. The decision she thought already made now was in truth, and whatever came of it she would deal with. "'Rizio. Come here!" The Grey Fox whimpered, clamping a paw over the wound in his arm and scurrying to her side. A quick glance told her whatever sanity had returned for that one instant was now gone. "Grab my pack." When he refused to leave her, Danica growled in frustration and slowly raised the Otter's head with the point of her sword. He blinked once, still moaning, and then his attention finally focused on her face.

"Listen carefully," she spoke clearly, staring down into his agonized eyes. "If that little spell lets you live, don't even think of carrying this further. Send someone after me, come after us yourself and miss, and I'll take my brother to the Avoirdupois. Or the Doloreaux. For his own protection. Far better for him to live long as a puppet than to suffer a short life dodging assassins. And then I come back here, looking for you, and anyone else I even suspect is involved with this little plot. So tell anyone involved. Stay...away...from us."

Perhaps letting him live would prove a mistake, but Danica felt she needed someone to send the message. Better to take the chance and get some use from the Otter. Besides, should Fabrizio be threatened in the future, she would need a link to the others involved, if any. The Pretender obviously knew nothing. Dead, the Wizard would be useless.

"Please," the Otter whispered, "just go. Please don't kill me."

Danica looked down at his hands, pressed against his gut. The wound would finish him, sooner than later. The magic must be keeping him clearheaded; he should be unconscious or in shock by now. Whether the Mage was deluding himself with the hope that he would survive the wound or simply awaiting her exit to heal himself, she cared not. Either was acceptable, though it occurred to her if he died the message would not be sent. Then I'll just find another way to send it, the hunter thought grimly.

She cleaned her sword and knife on the Rhino's cloak, sheathed both, and slung the battered leather pack over her shoulder. A quick glance at the bedroom door, and Danica wondered if there was a loose end here she might want to snip off. The fact that the Pretender was an innocent dupe, magicked into his position, drew the bounty hunter up short. Murder is murder. Her cheek itched; she rubbed it and pain stabbed deeply, the glove coming away bloody. Eye or throat, and he missed them both.

At a touch on his shoulder, 'Rizio turned from sniffing fearfully at the downed Rat and followed her out the door.

*   *   *

The healing bestowed by the Otter had kept Danica on her feet during the wild melee; now, with her shoulder pulsing thickly, the cool night air made her head spin. There would still be the guard at the gate. In her condition the bounty hunter wondered if he would prove too much of an obstacle.

She had to try.

A faint mist flooded the grounds, legacy of thick grass and ocean air. The damp, grey blanket deadened sounds, muffling her harsh breathing and the constant, thin whines from Fabrizio. At least the Grey Fox seemed calmer now, though urgency evidenced itself in his tight grip on her wrist. Danica could not stop thinking about how close she came to falling the final distance, turning her own brother, mad as he was, over to be slaughtered. *When did I go so wrong? Have I always been this way? Is this who I am?* The Fox could not say for sure, but was reasonably certain the answer was no. Most people started as bounty hunters wanting to do at least a bit of good - her words to Tucker.

As they slipped through the silent fog she recalled her first hunt; the excitement of bringing down the Bear who had killed three men they knew of, and most likely many they did not. 'He has a taste for it,' Mo-gei had commented. It was the right thing to do, the money they received a bonus, an extra joy allowing her to continue to the next criminal and hunt him down in turn. *When had that changed?* Certainly she had been an angry child, even a jealous child, but not a cold, empty-hearted creature. There were people she had loved: her Father, her distant older brother...and Fabrizio, very, very much. Somewhere along the path of her life that loving child had been killed, joining the many bodies the bounty hunter left strewn in her wake, and she wandered on without noticing. Danica wondered when that little Fox had been killed. *Killed or...*

Or driven out.

Sucking in a breath Danica interrupted her progress ward the gate, sliding up to take cover against the brick wall of the inn. Worried, Fabrizio muttered something and tugged at her wrist, but she shushed him. *It was impossible! If you take on a contract, you complete it. Finish the job. Carry through.*

Mo-gei.

The white Leopard had instilled many lessons in her, but always his most important teaching remained the same: the work was all. *Ignore your quarry's side of the story; right or wrong mattered not, they were already convicted. Forget about caring with whom you spent your time; as long as they held up their end of the work, they were worthwhile. A contract taken was to be carried out, regardless of personal feelings.*

Forget about being a person, enjoying life.

How often had she wondered about Mo-gei ignoring Malik's ever-more obvious madness? *The same way he ignored the flaws growing in me. To him, they weren't important.* The work, Mo-gei's work, was all-important, all-consuming, providing the satisfaction within himself to survive. When the emptiness of hunting people had grown in him, he replaced the dying feelings of carrying out justice with the satisfaction of a job completed. The Leopard probably tried to pass on that dedication to his two compatriots, knowing only that it made a life of hunting people for money worthwhile. But Malik already had his own, twisted reasons, and Danica....

Her mother was dead. Her father had not loved her. Tossed from her old life like flotsam, she discovered that in hunting others she could take control, something she had never before experienced, and thus care for herself as she thought no other could. With friends held at arms' reach and all other people divided into two categories, potential clients or potential quarry, life suddenly became quite easy to manage. Taking Mo-gei's advice to heart, she let the job become everything. But for a different reason :for survival, not satisfaction.

For control over a formerly chaotic life.

Mo-gei could not be controlled, but that fact did not affect their relationship; she revered him as her savior. Malik, her one competitor for the Leopard's favour, could also not be controlled, so she destroyed him by opening Mo-gei's eyes to the truth. I forced him to see what he had ignored. But in doing so she destroyed Mo-gei as well. His friend, his best friend, lived as a worse monster than many of those he hunted, far worse indeed than the children he slew. Any hunter of men for money stood only a few steps upslope from Malik on that terribly slippery mountain of morality. Could Mo-gei possibly be any better? Suddenly a completed contract was no longer enough to gratify. Doubt crept in, doubt about the right and wrong of the hunt, the guilt of the quarry and their eventual fate. Long before he suffered through his final agonies, long before he even met the prostitute who would kill him, Danica was certain any enjoyment, any satisfaction in Mo-gei's work and his life, had turned to ashes.

And it was all due to her own selfishness. Had she saved the children, had she confronted Malik herself, taken the chance, perhaps Mo-gei would have seen some hope in life, some true justice and moral justification for their work. As it was, there were only two dead children and a favored apprentice who stood by and let it happen. Thus did the Leopard lose hope in life, and thus he died. And a young Fox learned her final lesson. Never depend on others, for they will always leave you.

Danica slumped down the wall, rubbing the welling tears from her eyes. Had she tried to save the children, at worst she would be dead. At best, the children would have lived, and Mo-gei as well. Most likely the girl, Danica, would not have continued on the path that made her the woman she had become. Uncaring, rigid, and manipulative. Empty.

And now, she realized, despite all of her efforts, her planning, her crimes, she would die. She and her brother both. The mass of gold in her backpack dragging her down suddenly seemed pathetic payment for two lives.

With nowhere to turn, no allies, no safe haven,wounded, exhausted, and haunted by a necromancer's curse, they would be dragged down by their pursuers and slain, Danica's brave speech to the Otter notwithstanding. Even should she manage to escape the inn's walls, with their wounds weakening and slowing them, death was only a matter of time

Fabrizio pulled at her arm again, more of a yank than a gentle tug, and she drew back, suddenly furious, opening her mouth to snap at him. The look in his eyes, however, stopped her dead. Omnipresent fear and tension filled them, but under the dim, misty light from an inn window and the gibbous moon, something deeper seemed to stir. Far beneath the curse, Fabrizio de Rinaldi peered out helplessly on the world, unable to act or even communicate. Help me, the tiny spark, buried deeply, seemed to say. I can't think, can't act, can't help; I can't even speak to you. I have only one hope. WE have only one hope. You. The trust there gave her pause; after everything, all of the pain, the treachery, she remained his older sister, come to drive away the demons.

Gathering the shreds of her will together, Danica forced herself to think. In all Triskellion, there was still one place she could seek aid. With no idea what sort of reception she could expect, the bounty hunter was loathe to open herself up to more disappointment, more heartache. But the only other option open to her was to die, and worse, to let Fabrizio die. After sinking her brother in the mire, she found herself willing to undergo any ordeal to pull him out again. And yes, there was hope that at the same time, saving him would pull the Red Fox out of the life she had chosen. Danica would do something she had not in many years; throw herself into another's hands. Ironically, whom else could she trust, but the friends she had betrayed?

The Crested Mastiff it was, then.

Steeling her resolve, Danica shook her shoulders to relax them, wincing at the stab of pain. Trying to climb the wall would be suicide, even without an injured shoulder; gossip held that the tops of the brick were studded with broken bottles, and the frequent guard patrols would no doubt spot her and Fabrizio moving carefully over the shards of glass. The rear entrance, made for servants to take in deliveries and dispose of garbage, was a favorite gathering ground for beggars searching for table scraps; it would be well patrolled at night. That left the front gate and the Armadillo. In her condition, she would find it difficult fighting her way past a crippled work dray. How, then, could she possibly....

"I'm such a fool." Pulling her arm carefully free from Fabrizio's grasp, Danica slid out of her pack straps. One caught on the shoulder plate above her wound. A sudden, terrible roaring filled her ears, like that of the surf, and the bottom dropped out of her stomach. When the pain subsided and her vision returned she sat on the ground with Fabrizio, who alternately patted her hand and stared nervously out into the mist. Must be going into shock. Reaching out she snagged the pack and dug into it, finding the heavy pouch of gold aureals. I can't believe I didn't think of this. Quickly Danica pulled one out, paused, then grabbed two more. This was no time to be stingy. If the Armadillo wanted more, she could always give him the whole sack, but it would be better to start with three. Using the wall, she laboriously pushed herself to her feet.

The enormous man was dozing when they arrived at the gates, but his eyes popped open as Danica lead Fabrizio down the path. "Leaving so soon?" he asked, snide triumph creeping into his voice. "I guess you didn't have the package they wanted." Danica barely kept herself from shaking her head in disgust.

Why can't all Armadillos be like Porter? Quiet, polite.... "Look, we just need to leave, all right?" The guard stared at her, weak eyes trying to pierce darkness and fog to discern if anything were amiss. Though he made a perfect sentry behind a gate, before one the man's feeble vision was a distinct liability. As is his lack of a mind.

"How about I give you these," Danica continued, holding up two aureals, "and you just turn away for a few heartbeats. It's the middle of the night, and nobody will see."

The bounty hunter blessed the power of gold as she slipped between the cracked gates, following Fabrizio. She pushed him through first to avoid any chance of foul play, but the Armadillo, stunned by his good fortune, did not even pause to wonder why she was bribing with gold just to be let out without question. *Not too bright. But then, that was probably close to two months' pay for him, or more.* Glancing out into the deserted marketplace, lit only by the waxing moon, Danica sniffed the air briefly, scenting only the stench of the city after a rain. Nobody there, it would seem - no doubt there were people still moving about in the port, but fortunately not here, not now. Only the tents of hawkers and peddlers, their owners safe in their canvass fortresses against the threat of more rain.

Thirty paces from the gate, a deep, gravelly voice brought her to a shuddering halt. "You must be slipping, Danica, not seeing me here." Keeping Fabrizio behind her, the hunter slowly turned to face the Magistrate stepping out from the arch of a New Town doorway. *Downwind. Damn. I just can't stop making mistakes tonight.*

Umberto's clothing was quite rumpled, his eyes red and puffy; she supposed he had been awaiting her some time. Even his lace neck ruff was sadly dilapidated from the damp chill. It should have made him a ridiculous figure, but there was no laughter welling up in Danica. She glanced at his belt; a rapier hung there, thankfully not in his hand. She had seen the man fight once against a maddened criminal bent on revenge; the Ape was decent enough, and should she actually manage to win in her condition, pulling steel on a Magistrate was a serious crime. Not only the Otter's people, but the Guard, too, would be after her head. All things considered, she would be luckier to have to fight the Armadillo in a narrow passage.

And Umberto del Serio would not be, could not be, bribed.

"Earlier on I spoke with Luis. You remember him?" Danica shook her head. Umberto sighed. "The Skunk you bribed. My people are loyal, Danica. He came to me and reported the bribes - both of them. As usual, I let him keep them - it's my policy concerning such things, that the Guard let go certain small infractions to give me information hopefully leading to larger ones, and that I reward my Guard for bringing such items of import to my attention. The bribes usually suffice for that, and as they would take them normally, it keeps my men guilt free. In any case, I discovered a certain bounty hunter did indeed have business with the Don's son, despite what she explained to me before. This was intriguing, but not unexpected. I've learned not to expect the truth when dealing with her." Danica's already depressed spirit sank lower at his words. It seemed everywhere she turned, someone else held her, quite rightfully, in low esteem. "I was returning here to make my report to the Don-to-be," he began, placing both massive hands behind his back and staring down at his audience, "when who should I see but that very bounty hunter, one with whom I have dealt in the past, one who was asking questions regarding a Weasel but whose business actually concerned the late Don's family, walking into the very same Inn which I desired to enter. Possibly she, too, was avoiding the crowds by coming late? In any case, much to my surprise, she walked in with a Fox, a very well known Grey Fox, so perhaps she bumped into the heir out for a walk in the night air?" A thin smile crossed his wide lips. "But this Fox was dressed in rags, and behaved not at all like the man with whom I had spoken the night before. Indeed, one might think they were not the same person at all." Danica shook her head mutely; all she could do now was await the falling of the axe. "So I decided to wait. Now, I am not the most imaginative of people, but I found that while I sat in this cold dampness many interesting scenarios leaped into my mind. I confess most of them were of a somewhat ridiculous nature. For example, what if there were two Fabrizio de Rinaldi's?" Umberto must have caught something in her eyes, for he nodded then, as if to himself. "And if so, which was the real one? And now I see you leaving, bribing the gatekeeper, blood soaking through your cloak, and I have to wonder: are we back to one Fabrizio now?" Now the great hand was on the hilt of his blade. "Who lies dead behind you?" Danica could not imagine what to tell him, what he wanted to hear. Shrugging, she decided on the truth. He deserved it from her at least this once. This night is definitely a poor time to start growing a conscience. "Some people had accidents. None of them were Grey Foxes." It was a somewhat imprecise version of the truth, at least. There was no sense in directly incriminating herself, since the Ape was also taking pains to speak around the issues.

Again nodding thoughtfully, Umberto seemed to take in their position for the first time: Danica in front with Fabrizio hiding behind her lean frame. His mouth broke into a much wider smile. "I serve the throne, Danica, not the man. I care not whose fundament rests upon it, so long as the head attached to said rear rules wisely and leaves me to enforce low justice as I see fit. I feel this way for two reasons. Firstly, I am a simple Magistrate, with no control of Highborn courts and politics. I hold no power there. Secondly," he continued, ticking off his points on long, thick fingers, "chaos is very bad for my peace of mind and Triskellion's continued existence." An edge crept into his voice then, and Danica quickly deduced his meaning. No wish to see the Rinaldi at war, within or without.

"I'm just taking my brother here for a trip," Danica countered quickly, almost stumbling over the words in her haste to assure the Ape of their plans. "A long trip. We might not come back; this city has far too many accidents in it for my liking. I might even be blamed for some of them."

"Indeed," Umberto rumbled. "Perhaps that would be best." The bounty hunter almost choked with relief as it appeared the Magistrate was letting them go. "Your brother, eh?" At his skeptical tone her chin came up.

"Yes. My half-brother," she repeated defiantly.

His eyes widened slightly with sudden comprehension. "So? If that is the case, take good care of your brother, Danica di Rinaldi. And of yourself as well, I hope." Turning away, he began to shuffle down the cobblestones towards the Three Spears. "I believe I saw a smaller place back here offering some cheap ale in celebration of the return of the heir to the throne. If it remains open, I might raise a mug to the son of the late Don myself. Who knows, I may not get to the delivery of my report tonight."

Danica blinked back tears. Delivered, impossibly, from the depths of despair. Three times now. "Thank you," she whispered, and cleared her throat. "Thank you!" she called after the Ape.

Umberto paused, turning his head to regard her with a slight frown. Then he nodded his shaggy jowls one last time. "That is, you know, the first time you have thanked me for anything, Danica. You are most welcome."

She watched him amble away, so graceless in motion, yet with a curious nobility of bearing. The first time.... 'Rizio pulled on her arm again, near frantic with worry now. A drop of rain struck the end of her nose, eliciting a vicious sneeze. "Yes, Rizio, we're going!" She looked up again for Umberto, to thank him a third time.

He was gone.

Chapter Eleven

The cellar was dark, but a single candle shed enough light to allow Delaney to spot the spiders scurrying for cover, carefully eluding the growing puddles of water leaking in from cracked foundations. There were advantages to being a Raccoon. Had Armande accompanied him, the innkeeper mused, the horse would be nursing a cracked shin before long. The thick-set man set the bronze candlestick down on the nearest cask and began taking stock of his stores. Under the circumstances it was far from easy. He kept losing count as his thoughts slid back to the young Raccoon lying passed out in a bed upstairs.

Seven casks of the poor ale; some of them would no doubt go completely foul before they were drunk. They should be brought up, sold cheaply. What in the name of the Light of Truth and Beauty went on out there, on the trail? Four, five barrels of good ale; good for a while anyways, and then there would be five more barrels of the poor stuff. How did Tucker end up bloody well cut open like that? Three smaller casks of cheap brandy, along with assorted bottles, full and empty. He'd need to decant some off to sell to those who preferred drinking at their own hearth. What of the Fox? Did they even find him? One cask of the good brandy left, and one bottle of truly fine stuff; even Danica would approve. There had been a plan to crack it open when she returned, but that was looking less likely to happen now. Danica. What went on there? Dumping Tuck off, high-tailing it out of here without a single word to me. And nothing since.

He paused, staring blankly at the mismatched jars of homemade whiskey he traded for ale with local farmers. "How many bleeding casks o' good ale was it?" the greying Raccoon whispered. "Damn." This was a wasted effort. With his thoughts spinning endlessly around Danica, Tucker, and their little jaunt, turned battleground, Delaney lost track of the numbers as quickly as he counted. Had he even looked at the brandy yet?

Mechanically the innkeeper reached out, arms locking into place around one of the casks of soon-to-be-wasted ale. A grunt of effort, and his arms suddenly corded into thick cables of muscle. Flexing his knees, he hefted the massive weight to his chest and began the short walk up the stairs. Getting weak, old man. Soon you won't be good even for this; your back or knees'll give out. Staggering slightly, he wriggled the barrel through the door and slowly lowered it to the floor. It was vaguely disappointing that his only audience was Armande. Hasley, a dockworker by trade, one of Delaney's regulars, and the only other man in the common room, was occupied examining the underside of his chair. Blasted Elk's never figured out when to stop. Delaney supposed it would be another night in the storeroom cot for him, added to the laborer's tab. Where had the rest of the usual drunks gone?

"Get this behind the bar; we'll be selling it at full price in the morning, half by the night," he wheezed, leaning back and listening to the off-key noises of his back cracking.

"As you say," returned Armande, finishing the sweeping, and tossing the refuse casually out the window.

"Where did everyone go, lad?" There had only been a few left when the innkeeper started his trek down the stairs, but he expected them to be here most of the night.

Armande shrugged. "The rains started once again, and they each bought bottles and left for their homes."

Delaney considered this and nodded slowly. It made sense. Everyone in the city had been putting in some fairly serious drinking, first at the news of the Don's death, then at the fear and anxiety born from the tragedy, and finally at the news of Fabrizio's miraculous return. People were probably very nearly sick of ale, wine and brandy by now. And for the heavy drinkers, with the weather turning foul it seemed sitting at home with a bottle was preferable to a cup in a leaky, damp bar.

Well, for most people, he amended, staring at the semi-conscious Hasley.

"Put up the oak, lad. I'm thinking we're done for the night." Armande nodded and moved to the door, hefting the heavy bar. It was a formality, really, to keep out the beggars and chronic drinkers coming to look for a nip in the wee hours of the morning. The inn was a castle with walls full of breaches; any thief could gain entry in a heartbeat. But to enter was to risk encountering the innkeeper, and stealing anything more valuable than liquor required a thief to enter Delaney's room.

There had been one attempt. Word got out, and nobody ever tried again.

An instant after Armande dropped the bar into place, something slammed against the oak door. Delaney tensed, dropping into a crouch. It had the ring of a shoulder to it; could it be the Guard? A moment passed, and then a hammering began, rhythmic thuds against the oak barrier. Had they heard about Tucker? Crossing his mind came a mental warning that to fight the Guard would be to lose any hope of running an inn in Triskellion, even one as dilapidated as this one. They would find any way to harass and shut him down if he balked them, and if one of them were actually hurt, it would go much harder on him. But with the young burglar helpless in the back, nowhere to escape.... Well, I'd just have to make sure none of them reported back. Delaney flexed his hands, working the stiffness out of his fingers. It's been a long time since I've killed anyone. Funny how it's never too long, he thought sadly. I could do without that tonight.

Staring at him with a worried expression, Armande made a quick, silent gesture at the door. Delaney nodded. "Open it." He was gratified when the Equine picked up the broom in one hand first. Gratified because of the show of support; it was unexpected against what might be the Guard. But the bartender cut a ridiculous figure, thin broomstick held in one huge, shaking hand. Delaney knew full well Armande was nothing of a fighter. "If there be trouble, lad," he cautioned, "just get out o' the way." The Equine swallowed and nodded, then slowly pushed the bar up and away, having a rough time of it judging from the continued thunder of fist against wood.

As the bar was lifted, Delaney realized that the Guard would have stopped pounding a fair bit of time ago and started shouting, if not chopping with axes. And there was a faint tinge of desperation to the sound, an aura of frantic need. Then the door swung open and Armande stepped away with a grimace of fear.

Two miserable figures stood in the driving rain, vainly attempting to take cover under the leaking porch. One was cloaked, the other, taller figure wearing scarred leather and bronze armor and soaked to the skin by the freezing deluge. From their bent backs and wide stances, each hung on the very edge of exhaustion. The taller one raised her head and stared sadly at the Innkeeper, an expression of broken appeal on her visage. "Delaney."

"Dani," breathed the Innkeeper. Frozen limbs finally responded, and he lurched forward, forcing his body out of its pre-battle tension. Carefully he took hold of the pack, sliding it down her arms, noting her flinch as the straps fell from her shoulders. The other man, a hunched Grey Fox dressed in rags and wearing Danica's cloak, skittered back from him; the Innkeeper paid him no heed. "Armande!" he shouted. "Ye'll get some brandy, now! And the good stuff, mind ye!"

"B-but she-with the knife-and Tucker!" the Horse stuttered, staring at the bounty hunter in trepidation.

"Ye told me lad, but right now move yer bloody ass!" Delaney shouted, one arm slipping around the Red Fox's waist and drawing her into the room. The bounty hunter was almost boneless in his grasp. "And stoke up the fire!" Sliding her into a chair near the fire, the Innkeeper was shocked by the violence of her shivering. Is she in shock? Grasping her face, he looked into her eyes. "Lass. Can ye hear me?" Danica slowly nodded, never looking away, naked fear floating in her gaze. What's happened here? A spray of water spattered his back, and he cursed. The Grey Fox dropped the sodden cloak and sprang away wildly, stumbling over a chair in his haste. Danica's eyes abruptly focused.

"'Rizio!'" Her faint cry was fearful, nearly panicked, but the other Fox calmed almost instantly, slipping past Delaney and crouching in her field of vision. She let out a short gasp of relief.

Delaney began to unbuckle the metal plates on her armor, then paused, staring down at the wood beneath her chair. The water dripping down on her left was shaded with faint swirls of pink. The Innkeeper quickly stripped off the protective bronze on the right side of her body, then carefully began work on the rest. Once he started the wound was easy to see...a gash, high on her left arm near the shoulder. Clean but fairly deep. There would be no lasting effects, but if not closed soon, a considerable amount of blood would be lost.

"We'll have to stitch that," he muttered to Armande as the Horse handed him the brandy. "Here lass, but not too much. It stops the clotting." Danica took the bottle and swallowed a quick gulp, coughing violently as some went down the wrong pipe. Retrieving the bottle from her shaking hands, Delaney held it out to the other Fox, but he skittered away, staying just out of reach. Halfwit. Shrugging, the Raccoon put the bottle on the floor and the stranger darted in to grab it.

Armande arrived with a blanket and began building up the fire, so Delaney took the opportunity to head for his room. There he reached under the bed, coming out with an old, cracked box. Inside were a hodge-podge of collectibles: a broken tooth, a tarnished silver denar from years past, a lady's earring, and a thin, gold knife in the middle of the rest of the junk. If one looked closely, the nicks and gouges in the metal demonstrated its purity. Delaney pushed the clutter aside, scrabbling for a roll of oiled leather on the bottom of the mess. A heartbeat later the box was back under the bed, the Innkeeper striding down the hall.

Not content with only a blanket, Armande had fetched clean linens. Good man; he's only watched Desmond do this once or twice. Looks like he's picked summat up. At his inquiring glance Delaney nodded, and the Horse began shredding one into long, thick bandages. Delaney clucked once, motioning, and the Grey Fox hesitantly put the bottle back in his outstretched hand. "Lass, have some more. Ye'll need it."

She let out a terrible sound, caught halfway between a sob and a laugh. "Funny you should say that...." Another swig went down, then the bottle hit the table with a note of finality. "I can't be drunk, Delaney. I need to move on. Tonight."

The Raccoon eyed her suspiciously, then shrugged. "Your life. Though I can't say's I've ever seen ye in this state." He unrolled the leather, revealing an assortment of small blades, needles, and thin thread. At her questioning look, he smiled. "Had it made a long time ago. Hoped I'd never need it again, and now I'm cursed glad I've kept it."

"Desmond?" She asked hopelessly. "Porter?"

He shook his head. "I'm all ye have, lass."

With a shiver, the Red Fox turned away. "Go ahead." Even her whisper lacked life. The curve of her neck, the bowing of her head, it was the carriage of a person expecting a blow. Delaney delicately threaded the needle.

"Summat's eatin' at ye, lass. Why don't ye just tell me what, and we can stop all o' this cat-footing around."

Her eyes snapped back to his. "But...T-Tucker, he didn't say anything?"

"Nay." Delaney smiled thinly. "The lad rolled over on his side, put his back to me, and grunted. Didn't seem to want to talk much. Then Desmond came, gave him some herbs, and he's been out since." Waiting, he wondered what she would do next.

A spark of hope burned in her eyes for a moment, then went out. "No," she whispered to herself, obviously screwing up her courage. Then to him: "I don't know if I have time to tell it; I can't stay. I'll have to make it quick."

"Ye can tell," he replied, "but nae 'til after I've finished here, or ye'll be passing out in the middle of it." He snatched up the brandy and poured a good splash onto her wound, then more of the fiery liquor went on the needle as a quiet moan slipped from between her gritted teeth. Good lass. Tough as old dray hide. But not tonight; something had broken inside her, something vital, and Delaney wondered if he would ever see the razor-sharp girl he knew from before. The Innkeeper ran the needle through the fire for an instant, watching as the Grey moved to her and sniffed the wound. Danica pushed him away, but gently, without the abruptness she would have shown a few days ago. Maybe it'd be better if what had broken stayed that way.

The stitching went well; certainly the bounty hunter was no weakling. She bore it in silence, sitting, wincing, and chuckling once when Armande fled the room at the fourth stitch. Odd how some people could handle anything but a needle. Delaney could feel Danica's eyes on him, studying him surreptitiously, fearfully. *Exactly what is it Tucker will have to tell?* When it was done, he gestured at the Grey.

"He's got a cut on his arm I'd like to look at. And there's one on your face as well, Dani."

"Get the linen," she whispered, "I'll do his wound while you fix up mine. While we talk."

She rambled on while he bandaged her face and she tried to wrap the Grey's arm; she too busy to talk coherently, and he too busy to listen properly. She skirted the issue a fair bit as well, speaking more in vague generalities than specifics. Something about lying to them, manipulation, and being an all-around terrible person. Disgusted, Delaney gave up trying to follow it.

Stopping his ministrations, he took her face in his hands. The fur was now cut from around the wound with a tiny razor; it looked decidedly odd. "Lass. We're not a single one of us perfect." Seeming stupified, Danica simply stared at him, and he wondered if the words were getting through. "Mayhap ye've made some poor choices. Mayhap you're not the person ye would wish to be. But none of us are, and it's never too late to start trying. As much as ye can in this world, that is." The Raccoon dipped a small bandage in a bit of sticky glue mixed up from water, crushed powders, and some wax-sealed herbs that hopefully still held their potency. It fit securely, snug over the cut; the glue would hold, and the wound would not putrefy. The mixture served him well in days gone by. "Whatever ye've done, it canna be that bad. From the look of ye, it was turning away from the last step what got ye here, else ye'd not be feeling so guilty. 'Tis a hard thing, finding out your life wasn't the best; believe you me. But ye know, no matter what, I'm yer friend. Tucker too, when he comes out of his funk. He's young; both of ye are young. Ye take things hard."

"Talk to Tucker. Listen to what he says," Danica whispered, hanging her head, ears drooping, a fine portrait of self-hatred. "It's all true, and I just can't bring myself to say it. Then tell me I'm taking it too hard."

"Did ye do it, whatever it was?" She shook her head emphatically. "Well then." Delaney stood, looking down at the Grey's arm. "Not bad," he conceded. "Are ye sure ye canna stay longer?"

"We have to go, Delaney." Bleak depression hung in her eyes. "I might not be able to come back."

"Dinna be an idiot on top of a fool. Whatever ye did, people have short memories."

"It's what I didn't do," she returned, staring at the Grey. "Delaney, I want to come back someday. I want to see you, and talk to Tucker about what happened, and see Desmond and Porter, and even Seanna-"

"Shush. We'll all be here, one way or another." Rubbing her head with a scarred palm, Delaney leaned close. "I like my inn, so I'm nae leaving. But I'd like it better with ye in it. And yer friend," this last said with a flick of the hand at the Grey, who started nervously.

Danica choked once, and for an instant Delaney stood stunned, thinking she would cry. But there was enough of the old steel left that she swallowed once and rubbed her overflowing eyes. "Delaney, I'd-I'd like that more than anything. Believe me!" Still frightened, now some relief danced in her eyes. His words offered her hope. "Thank you. For everything." Abruptly a look of horror rolled across her face, and she put a hand to her mouth. While Delaney glanced left and right looking for a threat, she reached out and took his hand in her gloved one. "Oh, Delaney! Have I ever thanked you before now? For anything?"

Confused, he reared back slightly, frowning. "Such a foolish question, lass. Of course ye have - many a time." He failed to understand the mixture of relief and disgust that crossed her features then.

"Friends, of course." The word fairly dripped with annoyance, directed at herself he decided. She did not release his hand. "I'm sorry I've been-"

Delaney's other hand was free; he used it to cover her mouth. "Yer apologizing a little too much, lass. Ye need t' get going." Glancing around, he motioned Armande over. The Equine had been in and out the whole time; now he carried a pair of wineskins and a small wooden box that steamed slightly. "If one o' ye takes that in hand, ye'll have summat t' warm yer stomach tonight on the trail. It's a stew." The innkeeper glanced at the bartender for confirmation, and Armande nodded, glancing shyly, though warily, at Danica. She gave him a wan smile in return.

"I'm sorry about earlier."

"Ah, think nothing of it," he returned gallantly. Delaney snorted. Avoirdupois or not, how is it all the bloody horses act like they're king and lord? "Things were not going so well for you at the time, no? None of us are at our best, under such circumstances." He began to sweep low in a bow, but Delaney's rock hard arm across his chest stopped that before it fully began.

"Enough. She's having places to be."

Dancia nodded slowly and turned towards the door. And kept turning, all the way around to face Delaney, her face a study in consternation. "I almost forgot. Is Tucker awake? I need to talk to him." He could see the fear, and her mastering of it.

"I'm sorry, lass. He's out, and I don't want to wake him." Delaney scratched the back of his head, unable to stand her sad eyes. "The wounds were pretty bad."

The Red Fox nodded slowly, downcast. "All right, then." She shifted her weight uncomfortably for a moment. "Do you have something to write with?"

*   *   *

It was damned unfair, Tucker decided. In songs and stories a man wounded in battle became the object of sympathy, affection, and more than a little attention from the ladies. The lays were full of long descriptions of how honors were heaped on the injured warrior's head, and of the wellwishers sitting by his bedside. The stories never spoke of the queasy pain of the injury or the illness killing all desire to see even one visitor, much less one of the fairer sex. He had little energy, the fever having broken only an hour before. Simply lying in the bed sapped his strength, and the discomfort stole all hope of sleep. Desmond's herbs had worn off a short time ago, and the Apothecary needed to purchase more. Tucker happily, ecstatically gave the man money for that, but flatly refused to send a donation to convince a member of the priesthood conversant with white magic to heal him; curing people was the sort of thing the thief felt should be done for free. After several hours he began to regret his principles, but could not bring himself to give in. So the young Raccoon simply sprawled on the bed in a twilight of the mind and panted. *Heloise, either heal me or let me die.*

Over and over Tucker's mind replayed his journey, wondering if he could have done something different. Wondering if he could have handled the fight with the mercenary better. Wondering if he could have seen at the beginning Danica's true, hidden nature. Wondering if there had been any way to deal with Malik other than killing him.

Malik. A psychotic, brutal monster, from Danica's description, and despite his instinctive distrust of anything she had told him in the past, nothing he had seen of the Coyote contradicted that. The world was certainly a better place without him in it. *So why did I have to be the one to pull the blade across his throat?* Without the killing, Danica, himself, and Fabrizio di Rinaldi would all be dead. So what, exactly, had he accomplished? Danica was dead in every way that mattered, Fabrizio was a corpse or would be soon, and he was counting whorls in the boards overhead and wishing he could join the Grey Fox. *And for this, I've killed a man.* With a single, violent motion the young burglar crossed a line over which he could never return.

It was impossible to tear from his mind the memory of his hand dragging sharp metal through Malik's throat. He wondered if it would ever go. *Does Danica remember the face of the first man she killed? Was it possible to forget?* Though he cut the Coyote down from behind, it was too easy to recall his expression as the bounty hunter spun to sag against the wall: the shock, the horror, the belief in his own immortality betrayed. *Does everyone think they will live forever?* Tucker knew he himself had, until a short time ago. It was a lesson the Raccoon considered himself lucky to survive. Sometimes. Other times, like now, he simply wanted to get it over with and die. And for more than one reason.

Despite all of his disgust and fury at Danica, a good portion of the anger was directed at himself.

I shouldn't have thrown her out like that. For all of his long, impassioned speech on betrayal and friendship, Tucker knew he held some share of the blame. Friends did not turn their backs on other friends for making a mistake. Friends held together. The young Raccoon had not bothered to try convincing Danica that turning over Fabrizio was wrong. Instead, he simply let her continue and damn herself, secure in the knowledge that he was morally correct. No attempt to stop her by word or by deed. Am I any better than she? Is this any different than what she did to those children? Tucker never tried to help Danica find the right thing to do; the moment she fell of the pedestal on which he had placed her, the thief turned his back and walked away.

The door creaked open, and Delany's ragged face slipped around it. "Awake, lad? Time for yer liquid." The older Raccoon stomped across the floor, putting the tray down and bringing a full mug of watered wine to Tucker's lips. Though his thirst was terrible, the wounded man waved it away after a few gulps. Bitter bought experience told him too much would soon return, far more quickly than it went down. "D'ye need to use the bucket, lad?"

Tucker shook his head; his body sucked up all of the water he drank like a sponge, as long as it went in slowly. Blurry vision fixed on the tray. "What's that?" he croaked, pointing at the folded paper under the carafe.

"Letter from Dani." Delaney frowned at him, probably due to the sour look Tucker felt nailed to his face. "Boy, I dinna ken what happened to ye out there, but I think ye'd better listen to what she wrote It's short - she said she did nae have much time t'write." Tucker grunted and turned over, feeling childish but resolute. He would have nothing to do with that murderer. "Fine then. Ye dinna have to be facing me to hear it." There was a faint rustling, and then Delaney began to read the note, haltingly at first, but slowly gaining confidence as he continued. "Tuck. I wanted to say this to you personally, but Delaney is feeling moth...motherly." The scarred Innkeeper chuckled.. "What I put you through was wrong, and I am terribly sorry for it, and for what I might have otherwise done without your words. Perhaps when next we come to town you might be willing to speak to us, but that will not be for a fair while. I expect things are a little warm for us in Triskellion, but I promise we will return. Then you will get to hear me say to your face that you were right. Danica." The Innkeeper paused for a moment, and Tucker could hear the rustling of paper as he refolded the note. A moment later it was pushed, gently but insistently, under his arm. "Here." There was silence in the room then for a few moments as the young Raccoon considered the letter.

"Was she alone?" Tucker asked abruptly.

"No." He could hear the grin in the heavy man's tone. "Had a Grey Fox with her, a real prize that one. Did nae say a word, jumpy as all get out, and dressed in rags. Funny - she were real careful for him, but I did nae get the feeling they were together, if ye ken what I mean."

"I think I get it, Delaney," he replied drily. "I didn't think so."

"Does everyone ken the story but me?" the big Raccoon complained. "Both were a wee cut up, but nothin' serious. I had to let her fix her friend's arm; he would nae let me near him. But I did hers - that one was quite a slash."

Tucker stiffened, surprised. "They were wounded? How?"

A wide palm came down comfortingly on his shoulder. "Dinna worry lad - it's nae that bad; just a cut and a matching nick on her face. Painful, but nothing more. Looks like they got in a wee bit of a tussle." Fabrizio? In a fight? "Ah, she also left about half of the reward," the Innkeeper continued quietly. "Near as I figure it, that's about seven for me, by the deal we made. The rest," and the purse jingled, bounced in one of Delaney's huge hands, no doubt, "would be yers."

"Could you drop it on the bed?" Tucker carefully slid the note out of his armpit and held it delicately. "Thanks, Delaney."

The thick paw patted his head carefully, then smoothed back the fur between his ears. "Stop yer distressing, lad; they'll be fine. Just rest up."

When the door closed, Tucker rolled onto his back, staring at the familiar boards of the cracked ceiling. He ignored the purse; more gold than he had ever seen or not, it would keep. Instead, he unfolded the paper and studied the meaningless jumbling of letters. Got to learn to read. So Danica changed her mind; by the sound of it, someone had been less than pleased with that fact. More importantly, whatever occurred, Danica had come out on top. Or if not on top, at least alive. Perhaps Delaney was right. Perhaps they would be fine. Perhaps someday they would come back to Triskellion and he could hear the whole story. Certainly the thief was missing some vital pieces, but what he knew would suffice for the moment. Carefully folding the paper Tucker placed it on the floor beside the bed. His headache and nausea seemed to have diminished a trifle; to him, it felt like living in the Light of Truth and Beauty.

Be careful, Danica. She might not be the hero he once thought, and she certainly was no paragon of virtue. But her final decision had been one he could live with, and hopefully she could as well. It seemed, at the end of it all, she remained his friend. And, as it turned out, a better person than she thought herself.

*   *   *

The Grey Fox moaned in his slumber, rolling over and starting awake. Throwing off the sleeping wrap in a panic, he dumped it on the annoyed and groggy figure beside him, inching nervously away from the muttered curses. Crouching in the tall grass, Fabrizio laid his ears back and peered about with wide eyes at the grasping tree branches and the baleful eye of the full moon, glaring down from far above.

Danica stared at him blearily, chilled to the bone from sleeping on the cold, damp earth. We have to stop somewhere to pick up supplies before heading up to Harrogate... maybe a decent bedroll for two. "What is it, 'Rizio?" Recognizing her voice and scent the madman crept closer, trembling, the whites of his eyes showing clearly in the sullen glow cast by the coals in the firepit. "Another nightmare?" Tension drained from her and frustration vanished. "Come here." As he moved closer she picked up a long stick and poked the dying fire; it flared up, flooding the small campsite with light.

Fabrizio settled against Danica and she threw a blanket around them both. Shivering uncontrollably, the cursed noble clenched his arms around his chest. "All right. Sshh. Lie down." Nestling within his sister's embrace, the haunted Fox's fear dissolved into simple confusion, and he slowly relaxed, one muscle at a time. "Sleep, 'Rizio. I'll keep an eye out for dreams." Her poor, mad brother smiled faintly at her, nose twitching frantically as he tested the air for danger, and reached up to touch the bandage along her cheekbone. Danica laughed quietly, running her naked, ruined fingertips through the fur on his face, feeling the thin, raised lines around his eye and down his cheek that had confirmed his identity when she first touched them days ago. *Was that only two days ago, the three of us at camp? The lines of scars, dug by claws she no longer possessed.*

Her emotional storm had blown itself out sometime earlier in the day, just after dawn. At the inn with Delaney, and as they set out across the city, her feelings had swung back and forth between hysteria and depression. One of their precious aureals bought a silent exit from the gates, but an hour's walk into the night and Danica collapsed, at last giving in to a torrent of pent up emotions and tension. It drove Fabrizio near to panic, but gradually her sobs lessened and she moved them off the trail into some cover, where they spent the night. By morning, rational thought returned to the bounty hunter. Once again she was the collected, competent student of Mo-gei. Thoughts of her appallingly poor judgment and choices haunted her nearly as badly as Fabrizio's curse, though, and they made little progress in their journey north that day. They traveled cross-country both to throw off any pursuers and to avoid contact with others. Danica felt a desperate need to be alone, to consider her life to this point. Until now, it had been ordered, passionless, andempty. In a word, dead. Now there was responsibility beyond the work, someone to care for, someone who was helpless without her. Someone to care for her as well. The Red Fox had no idea what to do next or where to go beyond heading north, away from Triskellion, nor did she know how she would make a living while caring for her invalid brother. She was facing a fundamental change in her life; she found it simultaneously terrifying and invigorating.

Danica wanted to thank Tucker for planting the seed of truth in her and making her think about who and what she was. Still greater was her desire to find some way to thank Fabrizio for touching a part of her she thought long dead, for helping her to remember what it meant to be alive. Most of all she desperately wanted to thank whatever force or fate had brought brother and sister together after so many years apart. It had saved them both. *I guess,* she thought, still running her fingers along her brother's face, *I'll just have to do the best I can.*

"It's all right," Fabrizio's sister whispered gently. "Sleep now."

Raising her unpracticed voice, her memory straining for the words, she quietly sang an old, familiar lullaby to drive back the nigh.